DEATH ON DAMSON ISLAND

HENRY FLEMING INVESTIGATES
BOOK THREE

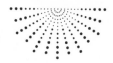

JAY GILL

VISIT WWW.JAYGILL.NET

Visit my website for new releases and special offers: www.jaygill.net

WELCOME NOTE

Welcome, friends of private detective Henry Fleming, I'm excited to share with you *Death on Damson Island*.

These mysteries are set in 1920s England and form part of a series although, of course, each case can be read as a standalone. In addition, within the pages you will find no graphic violence, bedroom shenanigans or strong language.

These stories are spoiler-free and, in the best tradition of the whodunnit, the cast of suspects, along with a smattering of red-herrings, will have you guessing until the very end, when our great detective presides over his *grand reveal*.

And so, let's pull back the curtain and reveal what took place on Damson Island.

Cast List

Henry Fleming (Private detective)

Skip (Fleming's four-legged friend. Yellow Labrador)

Mrs Clayton (Fleming's housekeeper)

Nelson (Boat Captain)

Charles (Actor) and Eileen Lockwood

Bea Arling (Actress)

Gino Sadler (Actor)

Leonard Birch (Playwright)

Randall Dobson (Production Director)

Norman Pottersmith (Talent Agent. Businessman)

Lady Mabel Garfield (Actress)

Audrey Warren

Joseph Timms (Actor)

An Extract from the Diary of
H. K. Fleming, Esq.

I have arrived on Damson Island as a guest of Mr Randall Dobson, theatre owner, director and businessman. The only residential property on the island is Damson House. A large, white, magnificent building, where Randall intends to continue rehearsals, and focus the minds of his cast on their forthcoming play.

From what I've seen so far, the island is desolate, yet beautiful. For such a small piece of land off the south coast of England, it makes quite an impact with its imposing cliffs and jagged rocks. Weather permitting, I look forward to some interesting walks.

The boat trip across was uneventful, despite the sea being rather choppy. It's apparent a storm is imminent and the boat captain, a weatherworn chap who goes by the name of Nelson, has suggested we make ourselves comfortable in the house and, metaphorically speaking, batten down the hatches.

Indeed, as Nelson predicted, the storm whipped itself to a frenzy of howling wind, that thrashed the heaving waves against the shore, lightning ripping the sky with ear-

splitting cracks, the likes of which I have rarely experienced. We are now cut off from the mainland and there has been a murder. Single bullet to the back of the head. Small calibre pistol.

∾

Today has been taxing. I questioned guests. Made notes. Once again, I find myself amid another grave and complex mystery. There have, however, been some interesting and quite enlightening insights. I must further question the suspects.

∾

This morning, I must reveal my findings. I am both shocked and saddened by what I must do here. As a student of human nature, it bears repeating that I am constantly surprised by it.

ACT ONE

THE CAST IS ASSEMBLED

CHAPTER ONE

THE TRAIN STATION

ENGLAND, 1923

Audrey Warren sat at a small table beside a window in the station café, toying with the white gloves in her hand. Today's meeting with Charles Lockwood had been something she'd longed for, but had repeatedly shied away from. Time and again she'd put pen to paper then, having read the words committed to the page, had screwed the letter into a ball and tossed it aside. Eventually, throwing caution to the wind, she decided there was no choice: if she didn't see him, she couldn't move forward with her life.

Sitting across the table from him now, she saw how silly she'd been. He was tall, handsome and blond, with the most piercing blue eyes. Slightly older than she'd thought, but that didn't matter.

Despite her reservations, she realised he'd been just as keen to meet her; something she hadn't anticipated. Now, in an effort to get to know her better, he was actively arranging to spend time with her, making her feel special.

'I've asked my agent, Norman Pottersmith, to find you a place to stay. So, go home now, pack whatever you need, and catch the first train back to London. But listen, Audrey, Pottersmith doesn't know about us, and I think it's better that way. At least for now our relationship should remain private.'

'I understand.' Audrey had eyes only for him and he for her. 'I still can't believe it! I'm so very excited about spending more time with you. We can really get to know each other now.'

Charles Lockwood placed his hand gently over hers where it rested on the table and stroked it lightly with his thumb. 'I don't want you to think for a moment that I'm not proud of you and longing to show you off. That's not why I want to keep us a secret. It's just that, as I'm married, things will need to be handled... delicately and, while we get to know each other better, the fewer people who know, the less complicated the whole situation will be. All I'm certain of is, that whatever it takes, I want you in my life.'

'I don't care about the secrecy. I've dreamt of being

close to you for such a long time and, now it's finally happening, that's all that matters.'

Charles drew his eyebrows together. 'I'm ashamed to admit, I've done things in my past that I'm not proud of and behaved in ways that were less than gentlemanly, or honourable. But that's all behind me now. I intend to make a fresh start and that's because of you. You're the most important person in my life. I've honestly never known a feeling like this before and I plan on telling Eileen, my wife, but I need to pick the right time. I don't know how she's going to react, though the truth is, I don't care any more. The only thing that matters is having you near me from now on.'

Tears filled Audrey's eyes. 'I really don't want to go back home. The train journey's going to be awful. I want to stay here with you. Now we've found each other, I just don't want to let you go.'

Audrey's train pulled into the station.

Reluctantly, they made their way out of the café and Charles drew her into his arms, holding her tenderly. 'You mustn't worry, I'll make all the arrangements,' he whispered. 'We'll be together soon enough.'

'GOOD HEAVENS!' Henry Fleming exclaimed.

'Oh my word! Is that *really* you, Henry?' gasped

Lady Mabel Garfield. 'What on earth brings you to London? An investigation perhaps?'

'Believe it or not, I've been sightseeing. You may recall my housekeeper, Mrs Clayton? I've been showing her the sights and now she's back at our hotel, quite exhausted. It seems she's only been to the city a handful of times when a child, and I think she's quite overwhelmed. Do you have time for tea, Mabel?'

'Unfortunately no. I've been running errands and must get home,' said Lady Mabel, looking disappointed. 'I've a young actress staying at the moment. She's performing in a new play with me that's due to be staged in the West End. Between ourselves, she's quite a handful. I'm merely letting her a room, but somehow I now feel responsible for her. She grew up in a small village and, when she first arrived, she seemed a timid little thing. However, the city's quickly transformed her into a rather wayward young lady.'

'Times have changed,' said Fleming. 'Is it a new play?'

She nodded. 'Rehearsals are underway at the moment, and we're set to open in a few weeks. As you know, I'd all but given up on acting; I'm not the young woman I once was. However, it seems the stage is in my blood, because when Randall Dobson, the director, asked me to audition for a central role, I found I just couldn't say no.' She smiled mischievously. 'I have an idea. Why don't you join us tomorrow for the dress rehearsal? You could bring Mrs Clayton.'

'She's catching a train first thing in the morning and returning to Avonbrook Cottage. She has an engagement with some friends in the village. Plus, of course, she doesn't like to be away from Skip, my dog, for too long. Lewis, the head gardener, is looking after him but Mrs Clayton thinks of Skip as her child and sorely misses him.'

Henry rubbed his chin. 'I myself plan on being in the city for a few more days, though...'

Lady Mabel beamed. 'Then come along after you've waved her off! You can watch the performance, give your honest opinion, and then we could have dinner. I know a wonderful restaurant that's just opened. It's been far too long since we had a really good natter. You're always so busy, and this is a perfect opportunity.'

THE SITTING room of Leonard Birch's small South Kensington flat felt comfortable and warm. Eileen Lockwood was tempted to stay longer, but knew that would be a mistake.

'Surely you don't need to leave right now,' said

Leonard. 'Why catch the train when you could stay here another hour? I'll drive you home later.'

'Charles will be home soon. He might ask questions about where I've been.'

'So what if he does? Tell him you've been visiting a friend. It's not like he cares about you.' He put out a hand and took hers. 'It's beyond me why you won't leave him. The way he treats you breaks my heart. You deserve so much better.'

She pulled her hand away and stood up. 'I should go.'

'I'm sorry, Eileen,' said Leonard. 'But you know I have feelings for you. I just wish you'd leave him. For your own sake, if nothing else. You'd be away from all his nonsense and I'd look after you, you know I would. It's what I want and, deep down, I'm certain it's what you want, too. I really don't understand why it's so difficult to tell him you're leaving. Charles only cares about himself, surely you can see that? Whenever he upsets you, you come running to me! It feels like *I* put you back together again, only for you return to *him*. It hardly seems fair.'

Eileen glared. 'Is that how you see it? Are you telling me you deserve something in return? That you've *earned* the right to have me? I didn't know you viewed our friendship in that way. What exactly is it you're expecting from me, Leonard?'

'I didn't mean it like that!'

'Look, just be my friend. If you need more then, I'm sorry, I simply can't give it. I'm married and that means something to me.' She walked towards the front door. 'I'm going to be late for my train.'

Leonard spoke softly. 'Please. Let me drive you to the station.'

She hesitated a moment, then looked at him fondly. 'Oh, if you like. I *do* care about you, my dear, but I won't leave him. It's simply something I can't do. In spite of everything, I love him.'

'I understand what you're saying, but I want you to know that, if you change your mind, the two of us would be quite comfortable, financially speaking, I mean. I have considerable savings. We could do whatever we wanted – travel the world, go wherever you'd like.'

'If someday I simply can't take it any more, I'll find a way, but I'll do it on my own terms.' She gave Leonard a hug. 'It means we must remain as friends. Do you understand?'

Leonard nodded. 'Knowing how he treats you is hard to bear, but I understand.' He took her hand and kissed it gently. 'Friends it is. I'd rather have you in my life than not at all.'

CHAPTER TWO

A DEAL IS STRUCK

'If you want my advice...' said Lady Mabel.

Bea Arling sighed and raised her eyebrows. 'Which I don't. Though I'm sure you're going to give it, anyway.'

'...you'll stay away from Charles Lockwood. Not only is he married, but he also has an unsavoury reputation as a hard-drinking ladies' man, a gambler and a filthy-tempered chauvinist.'

'Charles and I are just friends. We're going for drinks and dancing, then he's taking me for dinner. That's all.'

Lady Mabel frowned. 'D'you take me for a fool? I've known Charles Lockwood a *very* long time and, if I can promise you one thing, it's this: he'll break your heart and leave your reputation in tatters. Despite anything he might say to the contrary, he has no intention of leaving his wife. Eileen's a lovely woman who deserves better. For some unfathomable reason, she turns a blind eye to his love affairs and... numerous other shortcomings. Believe you me, Bea, he's no gentleman.'

'I've told you, it's nothing. We're just having fun. He's showing me the sights of London and there's no more to it than that.' She gave Lady Mabel a hug. 'I understand you're looking out for me and I truly appreciate it, but I'd like to drop the subject now. Please. If you don't mind?'

Lady Mabel wasn't ready to drop the subject. 'What about Gino Sadler? He's a charming young man and clearly very attracted to you. He knows London just as well as Charles Lockwood and, unlike Charles, he's not married.'

Bea shook her head. 'Gino's a darling. I'm meeting him and Joseph Timms for drinks too, before dinner with Charles.'

'A man like Gino won't stick around forever. Then where will you be?'

'You make it sound as though I'm an old maid. I'm still young and want to have fun. It's not like in your day, Lady Mabel. Times have changed, and a girl can do whatever she wants, with whomever she chooses.

We want to enjoy ourselves. Dress up, cut our hair, drink a little, dance a little, and enjoy falling in love.' She giggled. 'I need to get changed, and do my hair and make-up, or else I'll be late. I'm meeting the boys in an hour.'

~

RANDALL DOBSON and Norman Pottersmith sat in a dismal Fleet Street pub. Gloomy, with little natural light, the air was stale and smelled of sweat, smoke, and beer.

'The man's a complete disaster. And, in any case, the play's already too far into rehearsals. I can't change the lead now,' snapped Randall.

'Come off it! That's just an excuse and you know it.'

'Lockwood's unreliable. He spends most of his time drunk, chasing the actresses, and annoying the hell out of everyone else. I've worked with him in the past, and vowed never again. So, listen carefully, Norman, my answer is no. Lockwood will *not* be a part of my production. I want Gino to stay as lead.'

'Gino's a great young actor, of that there's no doubt. The problem is, he doesn't yet have the pulling power of someone like Charles Lockwood. You and I both know that it's Lockwood's reputation, including his antics offstage, that brings in the audiences,' countered Pottersmith.

'I'm not suggesting I would but, let's suppose, just for a moment, that I did allow him to take the lead role instead of Gino, how on earth would I tell the lad?'

'Leave that to me. I'm Gino's agent, as well as Lockwood's. It won't be pretty, but Gino listens to me. He has to.'

'Norman, what on earth does Lockwood have on you that makes you so determined to see him in the lead role?'

'That has nothing to do with you.'

Randall shook his head. 'No, I can't do it. In fact, I *won't* do it. This play has my name attached to it, and if it sinks without trace it'll be the end for me.'

'You worry too much. It won't fail.'

'Why should I listen to a word you say?'

Pottersmith smirked. 'Because I know about Mimi Wilder...?'

Randall's eyes widened with shock. 'Don't you threaten me with that! I helped Charles. Don't you *dare* throw that in my face!'

'Ah, but in helping him, you also helped yourself, didn't you?'

'I don't owe that wretched man a thing. We were even a long time ago. He knows it and so do you.'

'You lied, Randall. You might have ended up

behind bars, or swinging at the end of a rope. Instead, you're rich and the darling of the West End. I'd say you can afford to do me this favour; we wouldn't want the story to reach the newspapers, now would we?'

Randall scowled. He stared at his pint of ale and picked at the chipped table. 'This is the last time. After this we're done. I never want to hear from either you or Charles again.'

'Thank you,' grinned Pottersmith. 'I need this, Randall, and so do you, even if you don't yet realise it. Charles wants his career back and has sworn to be on his best behaviour. We both know that having his name associated with the play will have the punters flocking to the West End from all over. Once you've done me this favour, we're all fair and square.'

'You'd better mean it.'

'You have my word. And stop worrying. He's a changed man.'

THE CLUB WAS noisy with music, laughter and excited voices. The tables around the dance floor were littered with cocktail glasses and crowded with couples taking a rest from dancing.

'Stay for another drink. It's still early,' wheedled Gino Sadler. He and Bea Arling stood at the side of the dance floor. The back of his neck dripped perspiration, but he wasn't ready to quit just yet. 'Charles isn't coming, Bea. If he was, he'd be here by now. I'm a far better catch than him, anyway.'

'And so modest too,' joked Bea, pinching his cheek. 'Just one more drink, then,' she agreed, discreetly looking around for Charles.

'What do you make of our friend, Joseph?' asked Gino.

They both looked towards their table at the back of the dance hall where Joseph sat nursing a drink.

'He's a sweetheart, but I don't think this is his scene. He's also more than a little drunk. Just like you.'

'I may be drunk, but it's because I'm in love,' said Gino.

'Who's the lucky girl?' teased Bea, patting her newly cut bob and fluttering her eyelashes.

'C'mon, Bea, you know how I feel. I'm head over heels in love with you.'

'In love? Goodness gracious! We've only just met. You *are* a funny chap.'

'Well, I'm certainly a little in love. And I insist we have one more dance.'

'I can't. This new Charleston's exhausting! My legs are so tired I feel like my feet are about to drop off.'

'Oh, come on, *please*, just one more. Be a sport.'

'Don't you think you should be getting Joseph home?'

'Maybe, but only when you and I have had another dance. I really don't want to return to my pokey little flat and listen to Joseph wittering on all night – *again*.'

Bea sighed and smiled. 'All right, but first I need that drink you promised me. But it's only to save you from Joseph; he does look unusually down this evening.'

Gino's face lit up. 'You're an angel.'

'Sent straight from heaven,' Bea laughed.

He took her hand and recklessly spun her round a couple of times. She almost careered into a waiter carrying drinks, and giggled her apologies.

Bea gave Gino a playful poke with her finger. 'Don't go getting any ideas, though. One drink. One more dance. I've no intention of going any further. With anyone. I'm young, free, single, and out for fun.'

'I hope you don't think that's going to stop me trying. I don't want anybody else snapping you up.'

She shook her head and smiled. 'You don't stop, do you? Enough foolishness. You're drunk, and tomorrow you'll be embarrassed by your quite ridiculous proclamations of love.'

Out of the corner of her eye, Bea saw Charles Lockwood. She felt her heart flutter when he smiled and waved.

Gino groaned to himself.

'Sorry, I'm late, Bea. You look a million dollars, my darling. I hope Gino hasn't bored you too much.'

'Gino's been an absolute dear,' said Bea.

'Good boy,' said Charles. 'Make yourself useful and fetch us some drinks, will you? I'm parched.'

CHAPTER THREE

THE ISLAND

A dawn mist lay over the ground. Two men, in full military uniform, flintlock pistols held at their side, stood back-to-back. At the allotted time, each took ten paces, turned, and faced one another.

Lady Mabel Garfield, her face powdered starkly white, clutched Bea Arling. The young girl sobbed, barely able to watch as the two men faced off.

'Look away, child,' begged Lady Mabel.

'I pray that this is just a dark, merciless dream from which I shall soon awaken and all will be well,' wailed Bea, burying her head into Lady Mabel's shoulder.

The more mature of the two duellers, Charles Lockwood, focused on his opponent. 'Prepare to meet your maker, sir.' He proudly raised his chin, and then his pistol.

Bang!

The younger man, Gino Sadler, swayed unsteadily but was unharmed. 'You missed, sir! I have luck, and the Lord's blessing, on my side.' He regained his composure, raised his own pistol, took aim.

Charles Lockwood threw back his shoulders and fixed Gino with a steely gaze. 'Do your worst, then. I stand here for the honour of my woman and my regiment.'

Bang!

Charles grimaced but retained his stiff upper lip. 'A fine shot, sir,' he gasped. Lockwood staggered, dropped to one knee, clutched his chest and collapsed to the ground. 'An honourable way to meet one's maker.'

Bea broke free from Lady Mabel's arms and ran to the fatally-injured Lockwood. She fell to her knees beside him, her huge silken skirts ballooning around her. She clutched his hand, covered it with frantic kisses. 'Oh, my dearest. How has it come to this? Why must I be forced to choose between the men I love? No sooner have you returned from war and we are reunited, than you are cruelly snatched from me. It is a twist of fate so unjust that my heart will surely shatter into a million pieces. I cannot, I shall not, continue without you!'

'You must, my love,' Lockwood rasped weakly. 'For the sake of our infant child.'

Bea wailed. 'I shall tell the boy about the great man who fell this day. He'll make you proud. I swear it!'

Gino Sadler stood over the dying Lockwood and grieving Bea. He cast aside the pistol in his hand. 'You were a gentleman. A braver man I never knew. I shall pray for your soul and drink to your honour.'

'Fate has made its choice. She is yours now. Look after our love and protect her, as I would have done.'

'You have my word, sir.'

Lockwood's breathing gradually slowed until, finally, he whispered, 'How cruel is this? My life and my love, both taken from me.'

These last words hung in the air.

Impeccably dressed in a three-piece Savile Row tweed suit, private detective Henry Fleming leaped to his feet and applauded. His brown eyes shone warmly. 'Magnificent! A fine performance.'

The actors turned to the audience of three.

Agent and manager, Norman Pottersmith, sitting beside Fleming, and having seen the look on the director's face, clapped less enthusiastically. 'I suppose, it's getting there,' was all he could manage.

The director, Randall Dobson, did not applaud. He strode towards the stage, one hand on his hip, the other waving in the general direction of the actors. 'For heaven's sake! You're stiff as planks! It's all so terribly *wooden*. I simply don't believe what I'm seeing. Gino, you missed your line... *again*. How many times is that now? Have you actually read the script? Bea, will you *please* show some emotion? You're as flat as the Serengeti. These two men are your whole world, and one has been taken from you. At least act like you care, ducky.' He shook his head. 'This needs so much work. I don't think we're going to be ready. In fact, there's one thing I know for certain: at this rate, we're *never* going to be ready. This play, *my* play, *The Heart of Life*, opens in little more than a month. What *are* we going to do? I'm about ready to throw in the towel. I really am. I simply cannot countenance having my name associated with such... such second-rate tommyrot!'

Charles Lockwood sprang to his feet. 'Quite right, Randall. It's a disaster. A complete train wreck from start to finish. I'm not sure what more to say. We'll all need to work harder. I know Gino's doing his best but, frankly, his lack of experience is really showing.'

Gino clenched his fists but bit his tongue. He wasn't going to give Charles the satisfaction.

Randall Dobson now stood among the actors. 'Charles, Charles, Charles, you know I didn't mean you. I was impressed, darling. You were quite brilliant. My grievance is with the mortals with whom you must share the stage.'

Fleming, who had sat back down, looked at Potter-smith with surprise. 'I thought it was quite excellent.'

Pottersmith nodded towards the director. 'Randall's a perfectionist. He's the most in demand stage director for a reason. If he says it needs work, then it needs work. If you'll excuse me, I should join Randall to ensure everyone's content and on the same page regarding the work required.'

The cast broke for refreshments and Lady Mabel Garfield joined Fleming. 'I'm so glad you could come today.' Though she wore an outrageously large wig, and her face was powdered white as snow, Fleming could still discern his friend's attractive, mature, intelligent face beneath.

'I wouldn't have missed this for the world. As ever, Mabel, you were captivating.'

'You're too kind, Henry. In this final act, I barely had two lines.'

He smiled. 'You held this audience member in the palm of your hand with each and every word.' He took her hand, gave a slight bow, and kissed it.

'Now who's acting?'

The pair laughed.

Randall Dobson clapped his hands to get everyone's attention. 'Boys and girls, I'm afraid we have no choice. There are just too many distractions here in London. If we're to stand any chance of being ready, we need to focus, focus, *focus*! The drinking, dancing, partying and general flirting has to end. There's too much at stake, so I must insist we move rehearsals to my home on Damson Island.'

There was a general groan and some rumbles of protest.

Randall raised a hand for silence. 'I'll expect each one of you there by tomorrow evening. Norman will make the arrangements.' He delicately pinched the bridge of his nose. 'I need to lie down. I swear this play will be the death of me.' With that, he turned on his heel and sashayed from the room.

'I'm always up for a jolly,' said Lockwood, winking at Bea. 'As long as there's plenty of booze, I don't care where we are.'

'Where's Damson Island?' asked Bea Arling, looking confused.

'Don't mind him,' said Charles Lockwood, ignoring Bea's question. 'He always gets his panties in a twist if things aren't coming together the way he wants.' He pointed at Gino. 'Usually, when actors forget their lines, or are late to rehearsals.'

'*Me* late? You're the one we're always hanging around for,' said Gino. 'I didn't miss my line. You jumped in too early with yours. *Again.*'

'Come on, boys,' Lady Mabel intervened. 'Let's not argue.'

Charles turned to Lady Mabel and Fleming. 'Will you be joining us, Mr Fleming?'

'I wouldn't want to be in the way,'

'It would be wonderful if you'd join us,' said Lady Mabel. 'It's been too long since we've seen one another, and we have so much catching up to do.'

'I'd enjoy hearing some of your stories,' Charles urged.

Charles and Lady Mabel looked to Norman Pottersmith, who shrugged and nodded. 'Fine by me. There's plenty of room in the house. Let's just hope none of us get too seasick.'

THE SMALL BOAT lurched and swayed on the choppy grey water. Behind them, ominous black clouds had begun to gather, and a biting wind whipped in from the east.

Eileen Lockwood, who Fleming had learned to his surprise was Charles Lockwood's wife, turned to the boat's skipper. 'Are you sure my case is on the island?'

Nelson, the aptly named skipper, stared straight ahead as he guided the boat. 'I took all the luggage across personally, Mrs Lockwood. Along with Mr Dobson, the young actress, and your husband. I'm sure it'll be in your room by now.'

Adjusting her headscarf and dark glasses, Eileen turned to Leonard Birch who sat beside her. She spoke quietly into his ear. 'Now I know why my husband was so keen to get there early. He's *rehearsing* with her.'

Leonard squeezed her hand. 'Forget about him.'

She casually removed her hand from Leonard's when she noticed Fleming watching.

Audrey Warren, recently appointed assistant to Charles Lockwood, sat up and pointed as they rounded the island. 'Oh, look! There's the house!' she shouted excitedly. 'It's beautiful.'

Joseph Timms put an arm around her and pulled her to him. 'You're always so full of wonder, Audrey. You're like a big kid. We're going to have such fun.'

'And you're like my annoying big brother,' she teased. 'Though you do make me laugh.'

He grabbed her and tried to tickle her. 'Big brother, am I?'

'Knock it off, Joseph,' said Gino. 'Your clowning around's tedious. At least act like you're a grown-up.'

Audrey and Joseph looked at each other and burst out laughing. 'Yes sir, no sir. Three bags full, sir.' Joseph gave a mock salute.

Lady Mabel hadn't uttered a word since setting out. Her lips were blue, her face drained of colour. She breathed slowly and deeply. Seeing the concern on Fleming's face, she said, 'I'll be fine, Henry. It's nothing but seasickness.'

'We're nearly there,' said Fleming. 'You're doing well.'

Lady Mabel squeezed her eyes shut and winced at the sound of Audrey Warren's squeals of excitement as she caught sight of the jetty.

'Make yourself useful. Grab that rope and tie it to the piling,' Nelson instructed Norman Pottersmith as he pulled alongside.

Norman looked around blankly.

Gino Sadler leapt to his feet and grabbed the rope. 'I've got it.' He moved to the prow, stepped nimbly off onto the jetty and deftly secured the boat. He then put out a hand and helped everyone off.

'Are you coming with us?' Audrey asked Nelson.

'I'll hole up in the boathouse for a while. I have provisions for a few days. I shan't risk heading back to the mainland today. There's a storm coming in.' He pointed towards banks of thick, black cloud roiling over the sea off the mainland. 'I'll try my luck tomorrow, but I don't hold out much hope.'

'What if you leave tomorrow and we need to get off the island?' asked Gino.

He pointed to a smaller motorboat. 'In an emergency, you can use that. Anyone skippered before?'

Gino raised a hand. 'I've a fair amount of experience on the water.'

'Of course he has,' Joseph whispered to Audrey. They both sniggered.

'Good,' said Nelson. 'I don't suggest anyone risks going out to sea for a few days, but if anyone here's crazy enough to try it, then she's your best chance. You'd better make your way up to the house, and I'd better turn around and get this boat secured.'

Lady Mabel looked up at the sky, which was growing blacker by the minute. Fleming held out his arm, and they began climbing steps carved into the rocks. 'How on earth did they get the building materials to the top of this cliff to build a house? My legs are like jelly.'

'I can barely take another step,' gasped Joseph. Like everyone else, he was puffing loudly.

'We're there now,' said Audrey, pointing at Damson House.

The daylight had all but faded. When the front door opened, light poured out to reveal the elegant, fine-featured Randall Dobson filling the doorway.

'Here you are! Come on in, my dears, and I'll show you to your rooms. You can prepare yourselves for dinner.'

Damson House was vast and imposing from the outside but, on the inside, it was even more impressive. An enormous chandelier, suspended from the second-floor ceiling, lit the entrance, scattering glittering lozenges of light across thick-piled carpets, heavy wooden doors with shining brass handles, and ornately carved walnut panelling. Huge paintings adorned the walls and sculptures every corner.

Charles Lockwood, handsome in a dinner suit, waited at the bottom of the sweeping staircase. It seemed at first he was alone, but then Bea Arling appeared at the top of the stairs in a sheer, beaded dress and high heels. Her hair was now beautifully Marcel waved, her mascara thick, her lipstick strong and bright.

'You made it, darling,' Charles greeted his wife. 'Thank goodness. I thought for a moment the sea might have swallowed you up.'

Eileen Lockwood brushed aside his open arms. 'You expect me to believe you gave me a moment's thought? Which room?'

He handed her their key. 'Lucky number seven.'

'I'll be requesting my own room, of that you can be sure.' Eileen stormed up the stairs, glaring at Bea who was doing her best not to look guilty.

'If you'd follow me, I'll show everyone to their rooms,' said Randall. 'When you're ready, we'll reconvene in the drawing room for drinks.'

CHAPTER FOUR

BROKEN HEARTED

When Fleming knocked at Lady Mabel's door to escort her down to dinner, she insisted he went ahead. She had taken a nap to recover from her seasickness, and it would be some time before she was ready.

On the stairs, Fleming met Audrey Warren, and they walked together. Petite and full of energy, her shoulder-length blonde hair was a mass of wild curls, and she stared at Fleming with large blue eyes that appeared permanently wide and full of wonder.

'It's all very exciting,' she giggled breathlessly. 'Being here, I mean. I feel like such an imposter. This is my first proper job, you know. Charles has been brilliant. He's helped me enormously, and been nothing but kind and generous from day one. It's been fabulous getting to know him.'

'You sound like you're quite a fan?'

Audrey looked at Fleming vacantly, not seeming to understand. 'It's more than that, but we're keeping things close to our chest for now.'

'There you are,' said Joseph. He bounded up to them as they entered the drawing room. He enthusiastically shook Fleming's hand, kissed Audrey on both cheeks, then stood back to admire her sparkling gown. 'I see you've found Mr Fleming. He's a famous detective, you know. I hope he hasn't forced you to confess to anything naughty?'

When Audrey once again looked thoroughly confused, Fleming gave a slight bow and introduced himself properly. 'Henry Fleming, private detective, at your service.'

'Why would I need a private detective?'

'I swear Audrey hatched out of an egg only yesterday. So much passes her by. It's like she's in her own world most of the time. And I adore her all the more for it,' said Joseph.

'I suppose I can be a little naïve on occasion.' She shrugged and took Joseph's arm. 'I don't mean to be. And anyway, it's why I have you. You're going to tell me everything I've missed out on while growing up in the sticks.'

'Come on, then. Let's get a drink. Randall has quite an extensive bar and I aim to get squiffy.'

'Please don't,' said Audrey. 'You need to be up early for rehearsals tomorrow.'

'Haven't you heard? Randall's suggested we start mid-afternoon, to give everyone time to settle in, so I plan to get drunk as a lord.'

'That's interesting, and generous of him,' said Fleming. 'I thought the purpose of this retreat was to focus on the play?'

'It seems the old grouch has a heart. What's everyone having?'

Charles Lockwood was behind the bar pouring himself a large gin and tonic. 'What can I get you gorgeous people to drink?' He put out a hand to Fleming. 'I'm not sure we've been formally introduced.'

'A pleasure to meet you, Mr Lockwood,' said Fleming, shaking Charles's hand. 'I'm an admirer. I've followed your career with interest.'

'In that case, you'll know my life is full of highs and lows. Though I often think there have been more lows than highs.' He chuckled.

'Life can often feel that way.'

Charles nodded in agreement. 'You're a friend of Lady Mabel's, I believe? That means a great deal, and makes you a friend of mine. She's pure class, is Mabel. Now, let me get you a drink. I'm going to see if I can figure out your preferred tipple from your attire alone. It's a party trick of mine, helps me work on character.'

Audrey clapped her hands excitedly. 'I've heard about this.'

Joseph folded his arms and shook his head. 'There's no chance.'

'We know Mr Fleming is a celebrated private detective. It's clear he likes fine, tailor-made suits, expensive shoes, and I'm aware he served as an officer during the war. A policeman before that, presumably.'

'Quite so. A police detective.'

'A non-smoker. At least I haven't seen him smoke either a cigarette, cigar, or pipe, suggesting, that despite his stressful line of work, he's a man who feels in control. He also values his health over simple pleasure. Let me see...' Charles Lockwood ran a hand over the various bottles of alcohol. 'There must be some small vice he savours. Something of fine quality that, unlike brandy or rum, he might consider quintessentially British. Or, in this case, Scottish.' He placed a bottle of fine single malt on the bar. 'If I were to play you on the stage, Mr Fleming, you'd be a Scotch whisky man.'

Audrey squealed and did a little shimmy, shaking the spangles on her gown. 'I think so too!'

Joseph shook his head doubtfully. 'I don't know, Charles. I think he's a brandy man.'

'Which is it, Mr Fleming?' asked Audrey breathlessly. She bobbed up and down excitedly, setting her blonde curls bouncing.

'If I were to have such an honour bestowed upon me, then a fine Scotch would be most agreeable. However, I drink little alcohol, and on only the rarest of occasions do I partake. I consider myself teetotal.' He tapped the side of his head with a finger. 'This must always remain sharp. One never knows when it will be called upon. I'd enjoy a carbonated water with a dash of lime, if you have it?'

'I knew it,' Joseph groaned. 'I almost said teetotal.'

'Brilliant!' said Charles. He raised his glass. 'You make an excellent point. A great detective must always keep his wits about him. Unlike the rest of us.' He drained his gin and tonic. 'What can I get you all?'

Bea Arling appeared, and Fleming observed Charles giving her a less than subtle wink while he mixed drinks. He then poured her a glass of champagne and took her to one side. As they spoke privately, it was immediately apparent that Bea was not happy.

Gino Sadler, Leonard Birch and Eileen Lockwood arrived together, followed shortly after by Lady Mabel Garfield and Norman Pottersmith. The knowledge they weren't starting rehearsals until mid-afternoon was welcome, and everyone was in fine spirits.

'If you'd care to follow me, please bring your drinks. I've prepared dinner in the next room,' said Randall Dobson.

'I hear he's quite an accomplished cook,' said Bea Arling to Charles Lockwood.

Eileen took her husband's arm. 'You really have no shame, do you? At least act like we're married, as you said you would. You promised things would be different.'

'It's in hand.'

She didn't appear convinced. 'The very least you could do is behave like a married man.'

'Anyway, what about you and Leonard? You think nobody's noticed?'

'Don't be absurd. There's nothing between Leonard and me, and you know it. If we're to make a fresh start, you need to end this now.' She turned to Bea, who was following behind. 'Don't go falling for him, sweetie. I'm sure he's promised you the earth yet, I can assure you, he's going to drop you as quickly as you dropped that dress of yours.'

Charles glared at his wife. 'Not here, Eileen! I'll sort it out like I said I would.'

Bea Arling's face flamed scarlet, her eyes brimming with tears. She stopped and began searching through her handbag.

Having overheard the exchange, Fleming reached into his jacket and handed her a handkerchief. 'Miss Arling, would you be so kind as to wait with me for a brief moment? I seem to have mislaid my drink.'

She sniffled and nodded.

The other guests left the drawing room, leaving Fleming and Bea alone. They sat together while she composed herself.

'Thank you,' said Bea. 'I know you hadn't misplaced your drink. That was very kind of you.'

'My pleasure. It pains me to see a young lady in distress.'

'I've been foolish. Never in a million years did I think I'd be the type of girl to come between a husband and wife. What on earth did I think I was doing? I feel so ashamed.' She dabbed the corners of her eyes with the handkerchief. 'He's not even my type. He's blond and full of himself. I prefer dark-haired, thoughtful men. He's also old enough to be my father.'

'On that point, I can agree. He's certainly old enough to be your father. Possibly, even your grandfather. Though, not quite.'

Bea managed a laugh. 'I'm older than I look.'

'So is he.'

Bea laughed again. 'What should I do?'

'You're a charming and clearly intelligent young woman. You have your whole life ahead of you, and I have a feeling you know exactly what you should do. In my experience, these things rarely end happily.' Fleming got to his feet and put out his arm. 'Shall we?

If you will permit me, I shall be your knight in shining armour for the evening.'

'Why, thank you, Mr Fleming. I'd be delighted.'

CHAPTER FIVE

THE ARGUMENT

The windows, doors, and roof tiles of Damson House rattled and shook as outside the storm grew ever closer and more fierce. Lightning flashed, thunder bellowed, wind howled across the cliff tops, and rain lashed down. At sea, great waves were whipped up, and up, until they crashed, foam seething furiously, onto the jagged rocks and stony beach below.

In the cosy dining room, the lights flickered. Dinner was over and the table cleared except for cheese and crackers. For the most part, lively conversation drowned out the hellish weather.

'I've never wanted to be anything else other than a playwright,' said Leonard Birch. 'I wrote my first play when I was just ten years old. It was awful, of course. If memory serves, it was Christmas-time, and I'm embarrassed to say it was heavily influenced by Charles Dickens. I remember that having read *A Christmas Carol*, I somehow thought I could easily write my own Victorian masterpiece in the space of an afternoon. The idea being that my family would perform it in the evening.'

'And did they?' asked Audrey.

'Mostly, I think they were sick and tired of my precociousness, but my mother, always my greatest supporter, insisted everyone played their part. Which they did.' He laughed fondly. 'My older brother, my sister, my father and grandmother read the lines while I directed and rewrote things where necessary.'

'You might have been a director then?' said Lady Mabel.

'It didn't take long before I realised I preferred writing to managing actors.'

'You made the right choice. Actors are a thankless bunch,' joked Randall. 'Intractable, the lot of 'em.'

'I'll drink to that!' bellowed Charles. 'Where's the fun in living by the rules? It's not something I've ever done. Live each day as if it were the last, that's what I say!'

'I'll attest to that,' said Eileen. 'In all the years we've been married, I can't say a day's gone by when he hasn't surprised me. On occasion, there have even been a few nice surprises.' She raised her wineglass to Charles, then drained it.

Audrey laughed. Then belatedly realised it wasn't a joke.

Charles gave her a wink.

Norman Pottersmith sipped a brandy. The agent had been quiet all evening. 'As a boy, I dreamed of racing horses. I wanted to be a jockey.'

There was silence around the table.

He stood up. All six-foot-four inches of him. 'My mother told me I simply wasn't built for the job!'

The room erupted with laughter. 'She was right!'

At around midnight, Randall hushed everyone. 'I'm sorry to end the evening on a dampener, my dears, but, as the director of this play, I must address the reason we're here. In just a few short weeks, our play, *The Heart of Life*, opens. This means we have work to do. I'd like everyone to get plenty of rest and then tomorrow, after a hearty brunch, we'll resume rehearsals. Let's say a two p.m. start, on the dot.'

Outside, forked lightning split the sky, followed by a rolling crack of thunder. The lights dimmed.

Audrey and Joseph playfully grabbed each other's hands, squealing in mock fear.

'It'll be fine,' said Charles confidently. 'It's only a storm. We're safe enough.'

'I'm ready to retire for the night,' said Lady Mabel. 'So, if you'll excuse me, I'll see you all in the morning.'

As Lady Mabel rose, so did everyone else.

Within an hour, the house was quiet.

~

HENRY FLEMING HAD RISEN LATER than usual and taken his daily walk. By the time he returned it was slightly before midday and the guests were stirring.

The storm, which had raged throughout the night, had temporarily subsided, and a watery sun had shown itself. As he approached Damson House, he observed Charles Lockwood and his agent, Norman Pottersmith, talking. As he got closer, he realised they were arguing.

'God knows, I've done all *I* can. Do you have any idea how hard I had to push to get you this? Nobody wanted you, so don't jeopardise everything over some dozy slip of a girl. It's that kind of nonsense that got you where you are now,' Pottersmith seethed.

'Don't you *dare* lecture me!' retorted Charles. 'You're using me and I know it. Not that it's any of your business, but the girl's important to me and she stays. Have you got that?'

The two men looked up. Seeing Fleming approach, Pottersmith took his opportunity to stride back into the house.

Charles grinned. 'I heard you leave the house this morning.'

'My apologies,' said Fleming.

Charles shook his head. 'I'm a light sleeper these days. I seem to have too much to occupy my mind. I was about to take a walk myself. They say an hour's daily exercise is conducive to a healthy body and mind.'

'I've heard similar. I often use the time to order my thoughts for the day. Is Mr Pottersmith all right? He seemed a little agitated.'

Charles threw a thumb over his shoulder. 'Him? His life's a mess. Between you, me and the garden fence, I only keep him around because he's become part of the furniture. As an agent, he's borderline useless. In fact, if I didn't have so many problems of the female kind, I'd fire him. As it is, I don't have the time or energy to replace him.'

'Marriage isn't for everyone,' said Fleming.

'Marriage?' Charles frowned. 'It's not that. Eileen and I have an understanding. I play my games, drink too much, chase the skirt, as it were, she gets upset, then we make up, and everything's rosy for a while. Eileen's one in a million and there's nobody in the world I'd rather call my wife. We've been through a lot together, she and I.' He chuckled. 'No, sir. My troubles are far more complicated than the state of my marriage. If you're really interested, I'll bore you with the details some time. I'm sure you're a man who can keep a confidence.' He winked. 'I don't know about you, but I'm about ready for a cup of strong tea.'

'What about your walk?'

'I'll do it later. Or walk twice as much tomorrow.' He put out a hand and felt a spit of rain. 'I think we might be in for another storm later.'

As Charles turned to enter the house, Bea Arling appeared. Ignoring both men, she pulled the fur collar of her coat up around her neck and headed towards the cliffs.

'I'll be along in a few minutes,' Fleming said to Charles. 'I'll walk a little longer.' Charles went inside and Fleming turned to follow Bea, walking briskly until he'd caught up with her.

'Good morning, Miss Arling. The weather's surprisingly pleasant considering the storm of last evening.'

She nodded and forced a smile.

'I sense you're upset. Would you prefer to be alone?'

'I'd appreciate the company,' she said. 'I have a lot on my mind, that's all.'

'A problem shared is a problem halved.'

'After our conversation yesterday, I'd decided that today should be a fresh start for me. And so, last night, before I retired, I decided to tell Charles that he and I could no longer continue our... entanglement.'

'I understand. Do I sense this didn't go entirely to plan?'

'I was made aware that Mrs Lockwood currently sleeps separately to Charles. However, I didn't want to meet him in his room, so I arranged to see him alone in the library. I waited, but when he didn't turn up, I went back upstairs. As I entered my room, I saw a woman coming out of his.'

'I assume it wasn't his wife, Eileen?'

Bea looked heartbroken. She took a handkerchief from her pocket. 'It was Audrey! It's beyond belief. I've never felt so angry, yet ashamed and empty at the same time. How could he?'

'You're sure it was Audrey?'

'I'm certain.'

'It might have been that they were working. She is his personal assistant, after all.'

'I doubt she can even type,' Bea scoffed. 'She's as scatty as they come. I can only assume her *skills* are of another sort entirely.'

'I'm sorry,' said Fleming. 'I know it's of little consolation, but the truth is that it's for the best. You must move on.'

'That's easier said than done. We're all stuck here on this godforsaken island. If I had my way, I'd catch the first boat to the mainland and never look back.

However, I'm a professional, and this role is important to me. I shall have to rise above it all.'

Gino Sadler had taken Randall Dobson aside, and the two men were talking in Randall's study.

'You're my first choice,' said Randall.

Gino shook his head. 'You said that this time and look what happened. Charles magically takes over the lead role, specifically written for me by Leonard. He undermines and threatens me at every turn, and I'm not having it any longer. I didn't even want to do this play. It was you who persuaded me to take the part. Movies is where I want to be; they're the future, not the stage. Who's going to want to watch a play ten years from now? Charles Lockwood's a dinosaur. I, on the other hand, have my career ahead of me. My being here and a part of this production doesn't further my ambitions one jot.'

Randall groaned. 'Look, bide your time. Concentrate on this play and see what happens next.'

Gino thumped the table beside him. 'I don't want to wait and I don't want to work with him! You know exactly what he's like. We all tiptoe around pretending everything's all rosy when it's not. I'm sick of it.'

Randall ran a hand through his wavy, lightly Brilliantined hair. 'Let's focus on this afternoon's rehearsal. None of us will have a future if we don't stage this play. If it's a hit, which it can be, then you'll have the opportunities you're seeking. Have faith.'

'Faith? I don't plan on putting my future in *faith*.' Gino walked out of Randall's study and straight into Bea and Fleming, who were on their way to brunch.

'Well, excuse me!' said Bea.

Gino didn't look back. He ran upstairs where a moment or two later, a door slammed.

Fleming's head turned towards the open study door where Randall was cursing under his breath.

'He has a bit of a temper,' said Bea. 'He'll simmer down and be all smiles again before you know it. Shall we find a table by the window?'

'That would be delightful,' Fleming said. 'There's something magical about feasting with a view.'

Bea chose a table close to Audrey and Joseph. Making a point of putting on a brave face, she politely wished them both a good morning.

As they sat down, Joseph leaned towards them and spoke quietly from behind a hand. 'You've missed all the fireworks.' He quickly flicked his eyes towards Leonard Birch and Charles Lockwood, who were deep in conversation.

'It seems Eileen and Charles are incapable of being in the same room together for more than two minutes without trying to kill each other. I think Leonard's trying to pour oil on troubled waters.'

Bea shifted uneasily. 'I don't want to hear about it.'

Joseph placed a comforting hand on her arm. 'It had nothing to do with you. She yelled something about coping as best she could, and needing more time. Whatever's going on is big.'

Audrey's bright blue eyes looked down at the table. Her face and neck were flushed pink, and Fleming noticed her biting her nails.

Suddenly, Leonard raised his voice. 'Whatever you've done this time has really shaken her. She won't tell me what it is, but she's dealing with it valiantly, *as usual*.' He walked out of the dining room, shaking his head.

'It must be serious. Leonard always seems so placid,' said Joseph.

Charles clenched his fist and stared out of the window. A few moments later, he rose and left the room. To everyone's surprise, Audrey too excused herself and followed him.

Joseph raised his eyebrows. 'Those two aren't... are they?'

Bea didn't answer. She fetched herself some bacon and eggs.

'I swear this production's doomed to fail,' said Joseph. 'And there's only one man to blame for that.'

'It certainly seems there's a lot of tension in the air,' said Fleming. Seeing Lady Mabel arrive for brunch, he invited her to join them. She helped herself to sausage, a poached egg and toast from the vast array of items laid out in chafing dishes on the sideboard.

'I'm sorry to have invited you here. I'm embarrassed. All this drama, and none of it productive.'

Bea left her food mostly unfinished and excused herself.

Lady Mabel sighed. 'I warned Bea this would happen. I wish she'd listened to me.'

'She's trying to make amends,' said Fleming.

'I've known Charles a long time. I'm aware of the rumours, but all this... I had no idea... the way he's treated Eileen in front of everyone is shocking. I feel I should stay out of it, but I so want to give him a piece of my mind.'

Randall appeared in the dining room doorway. 'In one hour, we'll begin rehearsals. Have any of you seen Charles?'

'He left a few minutes ago. I think he was on his way to the doghouse,' joked Joseph.

CHAPTER SIX

A BODY IS DISCOVERED

The actors were assembled at the far end of the room. It had been built as a ballroom, but Randall Dobson now used it as his rehearsal studio, and for his exclusive Christmas parties. They had been rehearsing nonstop for nearly two hours.

Leonard sat at the back of the studio thumbing through his script, ready to prompt if necessary. He turned to Fleming who was sitting beside him and spoke in a low voice. 'I know the lines back to front. God knows why I keep looking at them.'

'We're all creatures of habit,' Fleming said with a smile. 'Is Eileen okay? I don't see her here.'

'She's packing her things. She plans on taking the first boat off the island.'

'I'm sorry to hear that. I heard she and Charles had argued. I gather their marriage is... tumultuous.'

'That'd be an understatement. It'd be far healthier for the pair of them if they simply divorced. They argue and make up as often as I change my shirt. It's a cycle that goes round and round. He does something unforgivable. They argue. She forgives the unforgivable. You get the idea. He recently lost their car in a poker game. Before that he sold her mother's pearl necklace to finance a party.' He shook his head and sighed with exasperation. 'Fortunately, I was able to buy it back for her.'

'Where do you fit into all this?'

Leonard looked at Fleming quizzically. 'What d'you mean, fit in? I'm her friend.'

Fleming nodded. 'I see that.'

Leonard frowned. 'Oh? *What* exactly do you see?'

'I see you care deeply for her.'

'I'm not sure what you think you've seen, or know for that matter, but you're wrong. You have no idea what Eileen's been through, and what she's still going through. I'll give you a piece of free advice. It's a private matter. Stay out of it.'

'I'm sorry, you misunderstand me...'

Leonard got up and moved to another chair before Fleming could say any more.

Norman Pottersmith took the seat Leonard had just vacated. He whispered in Fleming's ear. 'Don't mind him. He's a temperamental soul, and very protective of Eileen. He's asked her to leave Charles and marry him on more than one occasion. I heard rumours that she would too, but for some reason, she can't bring herself to divorce him. It's as if they're chained together and no one can find a bolt cutter, so they have to tolerate each other.'

There was a sudden commotion at the front of the room and the two men looked up.

'That doesn't sound good,' said Pottersmith. 'What's going on now?'

Joseph Timms' raised voice could quite clearly be heard. 'I quit!' he ranted, throwing his arms up in the air. 'I'd rather do just about anything else than spend another minute in the same room as this man.' He turned to Audrey. 'Are you coming?'

Audrey looked at Joseph and then at Charles. She didn't move or speak.

'Fine!' said Joseph. 'You've made your decision. I thought we were friends. I see now I was wrong.'

'Don't go,' begged Audrey. 'It's not what you think.' She looked desperately at Charles and then ran after Joseph.

Randall Dobson sighed with exasperation. 'This is utter madness. Everyone take a fifteen-minute break while I speak to Joseph. This is worse than dealing with school children.'

Pottersmith turned to Fleming and joked, 'It's not

always like this. Sometimes the cast doesn't get along and then the proverbial really does hit the fan.'

'It's curious that Audrey should find it difficult to choose between young Joseph and Charles. I don't see the connection. Surely it can't be romantic?'

'I've wondered the same thing myself. He seems to have taken her under his wing. I shouldn't say it, but he doesn't usually go out of his way to help anyone, except himself.'

'I'm getting far too old for all this nonsense,' said Lady Mabel. 'Charles certainly knows how to rub people up the wrong way.' She shook her head. 'I'm going to make a cup of tea. Would you care to join me?'

The room emptied, leaving Charles alone.

Fleming finished his tea with Lady Mabel and decided to take an early evening walk.

At the cliff edge, he looked out to sea. The wind had picked up once again, and the waves crashed against the rocky beach below. Overhead, ominous looking storm clouds had gathered once again and the light was fading fast. Lightning flickered, followed by a thunderous clatter. Fleming lifted his collar against the chill. To the east of the island, a vast swathe of rain blanketed the sea.

Back at the house, the fifteen-minute break had stretched to an hour. The cast had all but dispersed to do their own thing and it appeared rehearsals might not resume for quite some time. The windows that had allowed in some fresh air were now shuttered. The rain would soon reach them, and the storm would once again shake the house.

Fleming counted the seconds between the flash of lightning and the crash of thunder. The storm was fast drawing closer and would soon be directly over them.

Passing the sewing room, through a gap in the door, he could see Gino and Bea, who appeared to be whispering. Out of the corner of his eye, he glimpsed a figure moving along the corridor.

Fleming had decided to make himself a pot of tea when there came a wild, terror-filled howl for help from the rehearsal hall.

Fleming dashed towards the sound, where he found Randall in a high state of distress, stomping around in circles with his head in his hands.

Immediately after Fleming Leonard appeared, looking alarmed. 'Good grief! What's all the commotion?'

Randall pointed to Charles, slumped in a Director's chair, his head flopped over its canvas back. 'At first I thought he was sleeping. I shook him and shook him, but he wouldn't wake up! Then I saw the blood.' He raised a trembling hand to his face. 'Just here, beneath his nose.'

Fleming carefully examined him and, when he lifted Charles's head, he noted a further patch of blood at the back, just below the hairline.

Other guests had now begun to gather.

Bea Arling appeared. 'Is Charles okay?' she asked. Reading the look on Fleming's face, she pushed her way to the front, and staggered at the sight that greeted her. Gino grabbed her, holding her steady.

'What's happened?' cried Eileen. She ran to Charles's side and took his hand. Realising there was no sign of life, she sank to her knees. 'I'm so sorry. I didn't mean any of it.'

Fleming turned to everyone. 'I'm sorry to inform you that Charles is dead... murdered'

There was a collective gasp.

'Murdered? Are you sure?' asked Norman Potter-smith. 'He might just have had a funny turn. We should try to get him to a hospital on the mainland.'

'I'm certain. There's clear evidence of a bullet wound, right here.' Fleming pointed. 'It would be easily missed. I'd suggest the bullet came from a pocket pistol. A weapon small enough to be concealed.'

Audrey's legs gave way, and she slumped to the floor. 'Oh God, no!' she cried, clenching her fingers in her hair.

Joseph ran to her.

'What are we to do?' asked Lady Mabel.

'One of us must go to the mainland and fetch the police.'

Outside, there was a flash of lightning, followed by a clap of thunder and the pounding of torrential rain. The lights flickered.

'It would appear nobody's leaving until this storm passes,' said Leonard.

'Don't be ridiculous. The police must be informed,' Randall insisted.

'They'll be notified in due course,' said Fleming. 'In the absence of a police detective, I would like to propose that I undertake an investigation.' He turned to Randall. 'With your permission, of course.' He took out his pocket watch and noted the time. It was five-fifteen p.m. precisely. 'There must be no delay.'

Randall looked around at the blank faces of his guests, uncertain what to do for the best. Lady Mabel nodded encouragingly.

'I suppose it couldn't do any harm,' he said at last. 'With the storm the way it is, it would appear we're stuck.'

'I must have the cooperation of everyone for me to uncover the truth,' declared Fleming.

'You'll have it. I shall make quite sure of that,' confirmed Randall.

'In that case, I'll need to speak to everyone. I've many questions. I'll prepare myself in the drawing room and call upon each of you in turn. Firstly, however, there's somebody I wish to fetch to assist me.' Fleming's eyes turned to the window where outside he could see the storm's rage had escalated considerably. 'Unfortunately, I must leave the house for a short while. I'll begin my examination as soon as I return.' He left the suspects to fetch his coat and hat. Moments later, the front door opened, then slammed closed.

ACT TWO

TRUTHS, LIES AND A SECRET

CHAPTER ONE

EILEEN LOCKWOOD

I n the drawing room, which now served as Fleming's headquarters, two wet coats hung drying on either side of the enormous fireplace. The first, a finely tailored Ulster, belonged to Fleming. The second, with an almost overpowering smell of diesel, and a flashlight sticking out of the pocket, could only have belonged to one person on the island, the boat captain, Nelson.

During his walks, Fleming had observed movement at the foot of the cliffs and a light in the boathouse. Nelson, unable to leave the island due to the storm, had holed up there, isolated from the rest of the guests. Fleming, therefore, knew with certainty he was far from the scene at the time of Charles Lockwood's murder, making him the only person currently not under suspicion.

'First of all,' said Fleming, 'I'd like a word or two with Mrs Lockwood. I've a feeling she'll be able to shed considerable light on the lead up to her husband's untimely death.'

'If you say so,' said Nelson. The boat captain paused before leaving. 'You think maybe it was the wife that did him in, Mr Fleming?'

'At this moment in time, we must gather evidence. Once we know more, we can begin to draw our conclusions. Until then, you and I shall keep an open mind.'

'Right you are.'

'One more thing, Nelson. When you return with Mrs Lockwood, would you kindly sit here.' He gestured to an armchair in the corner of the room beside a window. 'I'd be obliged if you'd listen. I would be interested in your thoughts.'

Nelson left the drawing room and, a few moments later, he reappeared with Eileen. She was no longer tearful, but instead appeared calm and composed. She possessed large brown eyes and dark, glossy hair that sleekly framed her petite, feline features. She looked Fleming over, as though seeing him for the first time.

Fleming stood and offered his condolences.

Her eyes skipped around the room and then proceeded to take in all the details of Fleming's appearance. His three-piece suit, spotless, shining black shoes. His matching tie and pocket handkerchief. His greying hair, slightly receding at the temples. Finally, his eyes. A deep, rich brown that did not waver when her own met his.

'You've changed your clothes,' stated Mrs Lockwood, taking the seat indicated.

'Well observed. Appearances are important, wouldn't you agree?'

'I've been keeping up appearances for as long as I can remember, so I suppose you're right.' Mrs Lockwood appeared impassive. 'I'm aware of how most people see me.'

'In your opinion, how do most people see you?' asked Fleming with genuine curiosity.

'Some consider me foolish, others as full of self-pity.'

Fleming watched Eileen closely. Her hands trembled, and she fidgeted constantly. 'I, for one, do not.'

'I'm not sure that it matters now. I thank you anyway.' She gave a perfunctory smile.

'How does the death of your husband make you feel?' asked Fleming.

Eileen was taken by surprise at the question. She opened and closed her mouth.

'Did you understand the question?'

'Of course,' said Eileen. 'It just seems rather an odd thing to ask, and I'm not quite sure how to respond.'

'The question is straightforward enough. Does it

please you he's dead? Are you sorry he's dead? Do you have any feelings one way or another that he was murdered?'

'I'm upset he's dead. It might seem heartless, but right now I find it hard to shed more tears. I've cried rivers over that man for years and I'm done with it. It's not something I'd expect anyone outside of our marriage to understand.'

'Would you tell me why you were planning to leave the island?'

'Charles and I had an argument. I wanted to get away.'

'You implied in your own words that you've had many arguments and many tears, yet you choose this moment, just before his death, to walk away from your marriage.'

'I wasn't *walking away*. I've found this place claustrophobic. I needed my own space to think for a while.'

'Did your need to get away have anything to do with your husband's love affair with Bea Arling?'

Eileen scoffed at the suggestion. 'Bea Arling was simply another in a long line of floosies who, with the right words whispered in their ear, gave in to his charms.'

'This didn't bother you?'

'It bothered me a great deal,' Eileen replied stormily. 'What bothered me more were his lies, more than all his deceits, selfishness, and self-indulgences put together. Over the years, he's had many love affairs, but what I eventually came to realise was that they all amounted to nothing. In spite of all, I was his only true love.'

'Tell me about your relationship with Leonard Birch.'

She looked at him blankly.

'It's clear that you're close.'

'He's been there for me through thick and thin, and I'm not sure I'd have survived without him. However, if you're suggesting that he and I are anything more than friends, then you're very much mistaken.'

'Does he see it that way?'

'I've made my position clear many times. So yes, he sees it that way.'

'Can you think of any guest who might have wanted your husband dead?'

'Charles was a hard man to like. He had a habit of rubbing people up the wrong way. He was arrogant and rude, and his... lifestyle didn't sit well with some, so I'd say just about everyone here has fallen out with him at one time or other. You didn't need to know him long to realise the only person he truly cared about was himself.'

'Himself, and you,' corrected Fleming.

'And me,' agreed Eileen.

'Do you own a gun?' asked Fleming.

'Of course not! What an absurd question.'

'On the contrary. Considering there's one among us who has such a weapon,' Fleming said firmly. 'Why not you?'

'I find your insinuations insulting,' said Eileen angrily. 'If I wanted Charles dead, why on earth would I wait until I'm in a house full of strangers to kill him? Why not suffocate him one night when he came home roaring drunk or slip a Mickey Finn in his breakfast tea while he apologises for the thousandth time for having emptied the bank account and left me with nothing to pay the bills and put food on the table!'

'This is the question I ask myself but as yet I have no rational answer.'

'That's because no rational person would wait to be surrounded by so many potential witnesses to commit a murder.'

'Perhaps you're right, Mrs Lockwood.' Fleming motioned to the window and the storm outside. 'Did you hear the gunshot that killed your husband?'

She shook her head doubtfully. 'I might have heard something. A clap of thunder followed by a second crack of noise perhaps. It's difficult to say for sure. I was in my room. I'd packed my things and was ready to leave but needed to pick the right time. Not in front of everyone. As much as I might have wanted to humiliate him the way he has me, it's not in my nature. But, in the end, I decided to stay. I realised that Charles was right: it wasn't her fault, it was his. It was wrong of me to blame her.' She turned the wedding ring on her finger.

'Do you have children, Mrs Lockwood?' Fleming noticed her chin quiver.

'Charles and I weren't blessed that way. If we had, things might have been different. I could at least feel like the last two and a half decades hadn't been a total waste. I now find myself with nothing to show for the best years of my life. No husband. No child to love and see grow up.'

'You say you were in your room at the time of the murder?'

'Yes.'

'You saw no one? You spoke to no one? You heard nothing?'

She hesitated.

'Leonard came to my room to check on me. He'd argued with Charles and, knowing I was upset, wanted to make sure I was okay.'

'What did you say to him?'

'Nothing. I didn't open my door. I called to him that I was taking a nap. He apologised for disturbing me and went away.'

'You weren't sleeping?'

'No. I couldn't face him. I wanted to be alone. He knocked on my door again sometime later and I decided to get it over with. He can be persistent.'

'You didn't invite him into your room?'

'No. We talked in the hallway for a few minutes. I recall that someone walked past, but for the life of me I can't remember who it was. My mind's quite confused right now.'

'I understand. Please continue.'

'Leonard wanted to speak to my husband again. I didn't want him to because, as I said, I'd decided to give Charles the benefit of the doubt. Leonard wouldn't accept it. He told me I'd given Charles enough chances. That he'd never change.'

'I sense you thought differently.'

She nodded. 'I couldn't tell Leonard why, but Charles had convinced me that, this time, he would change.'

'How did Leonard take this news? How did he sound?'

'He was concerned for me and angry with Charles, which was surprising because he's usually such a mild-mannered man. I've never known him even to raise his voice. It was a shock when he told me he'd argued with Charles. He wasn't proud of it. On the contrary, he apologised for having got involved. He told me he hated standing by and seeing me get hurt.'

'I see,' said Fleming. 'Those were his exact words?'

'No. I don't recall the exact words, but that's the gist of it.'

Mrs Lockwood was dismissed, and Fleming stared at his notes.

Nelson got up and walked around, stretching his legs. 'Sounds to me like the poor woman has had a lucky escape. If you ask me, she's better off without him. Had I known the truth about that lousy, no good cheat I might have tossed the blighter overboard halfway between the mainland and Damson Island.'

'It's lucky for us all that you didn't,' said Fleming, not looking up from his notes, but continuing to write.

'What are you scribbling?'

'A few points to help me keep an orderly investigation.'

'Who would you like to speak to next?'

'I think I'd very much like to speak to Leonard Birch. He's clearly enamoured with Mrs Lockwood, though it seems his feelings aren't reciprocated.'

'Right you are.' Nelson put a hand on the door handle, then turned back to Fleming. 'Anyone who knows me would tell you that I'm better at reading the sea than people, but I have a feeling Mrs Lockwood didn't tell you everything.'

'Your instincts are good. She was most certainly speaking guardedly, choosing her words carefully.'

Nelson felt pleased with himself as he left the room to fetch Leonard.

CHAPTER TWO

LEONARD BIRCH

The playwright, Leonard Birch, at first refused to sit or even acknowledge Fleming's authority regarding the investigation. He was a white-haired gentleman, with round spectacles and a deep, rich, velvety voice.

'I've heard of you, of course. That doesn't mean to say you can simply investigate any crime you wish. This is a police matter and as such, I'd rather not answer any of your questions. Especially in front of—' He pointed at Nelson.

'I can leave,' said Nelson. He was in the process of lighting his pipe but got to his feet.

Fleming calmly gestured for Nelson to remain seated in his corner armchair. 'You're well within your rights to remain silent. I'm merely trying to establish the facts surrounding the death of your good friend's husband. The longer it takes for the police to be notified and to arrive, the less reliable the memories of all concerned. One can only hope the matter is resolved promptly, discreetly, and correctly when they do finally arrive. You may go.' Fleming looked down at the paper in front of him and made notes.

Surprised, Nelson glanced up from his pipe.

Leonard frowned confusedly. 'I had nothing to do with his murder,' he muttered eventually. 'Neither did Eileen.'

'Pardon me?' said Fleming softly.

'I hated the man. I didn't kill him, though. Eileen had nothing to do with his death, either.'

Fleming, smiling pleasantly, gestured to the empty seat.

Leonard sat.

'By telling you I disliked him, I'm being honest. I simply don't want to beat about the bush. You understand that?'

'I would prefer the unvarnished truth, always. However, it's an uncommon commodity in my profession. Those who claim to tell me the truth rarely do so. The ones who flat out lie often unwittingly wrap their deceit around a grain of truth. So you see, I must ask my questions, then chip away at what I've learned until I have my answer.'

Leonard grunted.

'Whose decision was it to cast Charles in the lead role?'

'Certainly not mine. I wrote the play with Gino Sadler in mind. When he agreed to play the part, I was pleased. You can imagine my dismay when I heard they'd made changes at the last minute and Charles was to replace him.'

'You had no say?'

'None whatsoever. As the director, Randall has the final word. I urged him not to do it but, on this occasion, my pleading fell on deaf ears.'

'Do you have any idea why he was so adamant?'

'I was as shocked as anyone. I knew Randall disliked Charles and so it made no sense at all. They'd worked together before and, by all accounts, it didn't go well. I know for a fact, he'd sworn never to work with the man again.'

'That's curious,' said Fleming. He was silent for a moment as he made a note. He raised his eyes and watched Leonard closely. 'You were nearby at the time of the murder, Mr Birch?'

Leonard appeared unperturbed, his eyes giving only the slightest flicker at this question. 'I suppose I must have been.'

'You arrived only seconds after I discovered Charles's body.'

'I was on my way to speak to him again.'

'You were?'

'To discuss his lines. After all, that's why we're all here.'

Fleming frowned at how unlikely that seemed but pressed on. 'Did you see anyone else before I arrived on the scene?'

Leonard closed his eyes as he tried to remember. 'I don't think so. I'd been upstairs and knocked on Eileen's door. She was resting and didn't want to be disturbed. I then went to my room, where I couldn't settle. I tried to work. I have a new play I'm planning but was unable to concentrate on it, so I came back downstairs for a while. I made tea. I waited a little longer, then returned upstairs and knocked on her door again. We chatted for a few minutes in the hall-way. Lady Mabel can confirm this, she passed us on the way to her room. After our conversation, I wanted to talk to Charles, but I needed a moment to consider my words so, instead of going to see him immediately, I went to the kitchen to get a bite to eat; I get hungry when I'm anxious. That's when I heard Randall call out.'

'You saw no one else? You heard nothing before Randall's plea for help?'

Leonard shook his head. He then appeared to remember something. 'The door in the kitchen that opens to the outside—'

'What about it?'

'It was open. I mean wide open. I hadn't thought about it until now. It seemed odd. I assumed the wind had somehow caught it.'

'That's quite possible,' said Fleming. 'It is also quite possible that somebody went that way to dispose of the murder weapon. I must look immediately.'

'But what about the storm?' said Leonard. 'Surely it would be better to wait until morning.'

'Morning might be too late. If the weapon was discarded in haste, there may be a clue to the identity of our killer.'

Fleming rose and instructed Nelson to follow him. 'Thank you, Leonard, you are dismissed.'

The two men grabbed their coats and moved with urgency to the back of the house, through the kitchen and out into the stormy evening. Nelson switched on his flashlight. Fleming held aloft a lantern retrieved from the cloakroom. The two men peered into the gloom, needles of rain lashing their faces, thunder and lightning battling it out overhead. Having first followed the garden path, they moved separately onto the lawn where the ground became soft underfoot. The smell of mud and salty ocean spray filled their nostrils.

'What are we looking for?' yelled Nelson.

Fleming didn't answer. His keen eyes scoured the

lawn. A low wall skirted the lawn's perimeter; the garden appeared to be divided into sections. Fleming felt the whip of an apple tree branch. Ahead of him, an urn had been overturned and smashed. He squinted as he saw movement; held up the lantern, sweeping it from left to right.

'Is that you, Nelson?'

There was no reply, the sound of his voice lost in the storm.

Overhead, lightning flashed. Fleming spun to his right. Outside the garden wall, towards the cliff, he fleetingly glimpsed a figure moving in the darkness lit briefly by the flash of light, then gone.

'Nelson!' shouted Fleming.

'Have you found something?' came Nelson's gruff, breathless voice. He stood beside him, wiping rain from his eyes and peering into the blackness. 'You look like you've seen a ghost, Mr Fleming?'

'No ghost, Nelson, the figure I saw was very real and I fear we're too late. Our killer got wind of our search and better disposed of the weapon. Most likely tossing it over the cliff's edge. We should return to the house.'

'Suits me,' said Nelson. 'This is the wrong night for a garden party!'

CHAPTER THREE

GINO SADLER

Gino Sadler arrived full of confidence and bravado. His features were dark, his face handsome with sharp cheekbones above a square jaw. His hair had a natural wave which gleamed with pomade. He smoothed the thin moustache between his strong nose and full lips.

'Ask away,' he said. He offered Fleming and Nelson a cigarette, which was declined. 'I'm guessing you want to know where I was when Charles got his comeuppance? Well, I'll tell you. I was in the sewing room going through my lines.' He struck a match and took his time lighting his cigarette, as though the task were a ritual that had to be exact.

'Was anyone with you?' asked Fleming.

'I was alone.' Then added, 'Well, no. Actually, Bea was there too. She was subdued and didn't say much.

Before you get all excited and pin his demise on me, the door was open and I saw at least two people pass by. Certainly one of them must have seen either me or Bea.'

'Are you able to recall who passed by?'

'Unfortunately, no. I might have seen Joseph, though I can't be sure.'

'Two people, you say?'

'At least.'

'Could it have been the same person going back and forth?'

Gino thought for a moment. 'I suppose it might have been.' His confidence diminished. 'Whoever it was moved at speed. Each time I heard a noise, by the time I looked up, they were gone. To be honest, I wasn't really paying much attention.'

'You didn't think it odd that someone was running past the door.'

'I didn't say they were *running*. They were moving in haste but still at a walking pace.'

Fleming appeared pleased with himself. 'Thank you. These little details matter. You didn't think to go to the door?'

'Why should I? I had no idea ol' Charlie was getting his brains blown out,' Gino said cheerfully.

Fleming was not amused but encouraged Gino's frankness.

'Did either you or Bea leave the sewing room before the murder?'

'I don't think so.'

'You didn't or you're uncertain?'

'Uncertain. I might have gone for a cuppa. Bea certainly went outside for a moment. I think she may have wanted a cigarette. I do recall taking a fleeting look out of the sewing room window and seeing her in the garden. At the time, I didn't know I was going to need an alibi. If I had, I might have taken notes.'

'Let's move on. I understand you and Charles didn't see eye to eye.'

'I don't know why you'd say that.'

'My understanding is that you were the play's lead until Randall replaced you with Charles.'

Gino attempted to appear unmoved, but a brief tightening of his mouth betrayed him.

'It's no big deal. That sort of thing happens more than you might think. I'm a young actor, I've years ahead of me. While Charles, on the other hand...' He put two fingers to his head and pretended to pull a trigger. 'All this is irrelevant now, isn't it? I imagine the play's opening date will have to be postponed.' He shrugged.

'Had you worked with Charles in the past?'

'No. Acting is a tough way to make a living. Like most of us here, I have spells when I perform and then times when I return to the day job. I'm actually a qualified solicitor. My father owns a firm in Kent, Sadler and Sons Solicitors. It's quite a mouthful, I know. My twin brother works there too. My father insisted that I study first and immediately afterwards join the family business. Then, and only then, would he countenance me following my dream. The family tolerate my acting ambitions and allow me time off to pursue them.

'I can't blame the old man,' continued Gino. 'The truth is, he was right. Financially speaking, acting's a precarious profession. Few can support themselves, let alone a family. The desire to perform on the stage must be in the blood, or else one wouldn't do it.'

'Am I correct in thinking you and your family had no connections within the theatrical profession?'

'None,' said Gino proudly.

Fleming looked thoughtful. 'Yet here you are. Working with the likes of Randall Dobson and Leonard Birch.'

'Talent goes a long way.'

'In my experience, talent gets you only so far. After which ambition, drive and a willingness to, shall we say, step over people, is required.'

Gino appeared puzzled. 'I've never experienced anything like that. I shall have to take your word for it. You seem to have all the answers.'

'On the contrary, Mr Sadler. I have few answers. What I do have though are many questions,' said Fleming seriously. 'You see, I know that you show little regard for the fact you were removed as lead actor in this, a pivotal play in your career. A play scheduled to debut in the West End, no less. I'm also aware of your ambition to move into the emerging film industry. Naturally, an exciting prospect for a young man such as yourself. Therefore, I ask myself, why would you pretend to me that you don't care? What does Mr Gino Sadler wish to hide? After all, is it not human nature to be angry, frustrated, even furious when a big opportunity is snatched from one's grasp by an undeserving rival?'

'Charles Lockwood is hardly undeserving,' said Gino.

'Then he deserved it more than you, perhaps?'

'I wouldn't say that.'

'No...? Charles, a talented and respected actor, would surely deserve the role more than an upcoming and, some might say, unknown actor such as yourself. Whereas, a man of Charles's influence, again unlike yourself, could probably snap his fingers and demand the role.'

'I'm not unknown.'

'Of course.'

'I'm *not* unknown,' repeated Gino.

'You worked hard to get the lead role. Sacrificed so much.'

'There will be more opportunities.'

'Even though it's now known you were usurped by an ageing and unlikeable character, such as Charles?'

'I didn't say he was unlikeable.'

'You didn't need to. I can gather that for myself. I doubt many here on this island were fond of him. Yet, for some reason, he was still able to take away from you something you've worked so hard for. Are you suggesting there might be another reason he got the role? If not, then that leaves the only other explanation being that you *are* relatively unknown, that his name on the billboards will sell more tickets at the box office. You share the same agent. Why would Norman Potter-smith insist Charles have the role if not for the fact he considered him more talented than you? Or they didn't want to risk opening the show with an unknown name as lead.'

Gino's fists were so tightly clenched that his knuckles showed white against his skin. 'Pottersmith had no choice! Charles blackmailed him.'

'Aha!' said Fleming with satisfaction. 'Finally some truth. How did Charles blackmail Norman?'

Gino stared out the window. He was deep in thought. 'That's something I don't know. I wish I did but I don't. When I argued with Pottersmith, which I freely admit I did, at the injustice of Charles replacing me, he told me he had no choice, that Charles could have the whole play shut down and ruin us all. Randall and Leonard included.'

'Do you think he was telling the truth?'

'I don't know,' sighed Gino. 'Who can you believe?'

'That's a question I ask myself more often than I care to.' Fleming got to his feet and stretched his legs. 'That's all for now.'

The door closed behind Gino.

Nelson puffed on his pipe and chuckled. 'That got a little heated. I thought you might lose your rag at one point there.'

'Human nature is a curious thing. There are those who are keen to share what they know, but for them to be able to do so, they must believe they're left with no choice. My instincts told me Gino had information to share, but his pride wouldn't allow him to reveal it without prompting. And so, we played our little game until he felt ready.'

CHAPTER FOUR

JOSEPH TIMMS

Joseph Timms sat stiffly in the chair opposite Fleming. Like a bird on a perch, his body moved and twitched in short, sharp jerks, while his small, dark eyes darted around the room, alert both to movement and his surroundings. He picked nervously at his teeth with a thumbnail.

'There's no need to be concerned,' said Fleming soothingly. 'I merely wish to ask you a few simple questions.'

'I heard raised voices when Gino was sitting where I am now?'

'Mr Sadler was, at times, vocal. This is true. He required a little encouragement before he was willing to cooperate. Which, under these unusual circum-stances, is quite understandable. In the end, he was very helpful, and I believe we parted on good terms. I sense, however, you are of a more obliging nature. Keen to assist the enquiry.'

His head bobbed from side to side as if unsure whether to nod in agreement or shake it in denial. 'I'm definitely here to help in any way I can,' he said at last. 'It's horrible what's happened and I want all this behind me. All I ever want is an easy life and to have fun.'

'You're one of life's jokers?' suggested Fleming. He remembered the young man who had laughed and joked with Audrey on the boat to the island.

Joseph smiled, his nervousness fading slightly as he spoke with enthusiasm. 'I like to make people smile, always have done. There's no better feeling in the world than giving someone the joy of laughter. With a gesture, an action, or a few choice words, you're able to make their day better. Right now, though, I feel scared and I don't like it.'

'Besides Charles's murder, do have any reason to be scared?'

He shook his head. 'I'm not a brave person, Mr Fleming. My mother says I've been delicate since the day I was born.'

'I sense you have a cautious and protective nature.'

He put a hand to his heart. 'It's true. I've been comforting Audrey. She seems shaken by what's happened.'

'You appear to have struck up quite a close friend-ship with Audrey.'

His eyes widened. 'She's devastated by Charles's death. I've never seen anyone so distraught.'

'How does that make you feel?'

He looked blankly at Fleming. 'I don't know. Confused? They talked a lot, which I found peculiar, as I couldn't see what they could possibly have in common. I worried he was trying to, you know... seduce her... but she told me it wasn't like that. In fact, she was adamant there could never be anything of that kind between them. I'm not sure I believed her.'

'That's interesting,' said Fleming. 'How did she describe their relationship?'

'Friends,' he said flatly.

'Let's turn to the murder itself. Did you hear or see anything at the time, or notice something out of the ordinary prior to the death?'

'Nothing. I thought we were all getting along just dandy. Who could have had any idea something like this was lurking around the corner. I wouldn't have come to the island had I known. It's not like anyone would miss me. My part in the play's very small.'

'Without wishing to offend, I myself wondered why it was that you travelled all this way. Surely, it's only necessary for the lead actors, who have many lines to rehearse.'

'That's what I told Norman, Mr Pottersmith, but he insisted I come.' He smiled. 'So here I am. Looking on the bright side, I've been able to keep Audrey company. She's become a good friend. Though I really would like to leave the island at the earliest possibility.' Outside, the wind howled and rain lashed the window. 'Though it looks like we're stuck here for now.'

'Nobody's leaving the island for a day or two,' agreed Nelson. He stood by the window, gazing out into the darkness.

Joseph thought the partially-silhouetted Nelson, the haggard seafarer trapped on land, resembled a figure full of longing and melancholy in a dark oil painting. 'The funny thing is, I was about to catch a boat to America when Mr Pottersmith persuaded me to audition for this play. I thought there may be opportunities for an Englishman abroad, that I might perhaps stand out more at auditions. Right now, I could have been in Hollywood. Charlie Chaplin's English, of course. I'm not suggesting I could be as big a name as him, but there's still success to be had. You just need luck and an agent who believes in you.'

'America's a big place to go it alone. Do you have contacts out there?' asked Fleming with concern.

'None to speak of. I thought I'd just hop off the boat and head towards the bright lights, with nothing more than a few dollars in my pocket and a heart full of dreams and ambition.'

'If you don't mind my saying, that seems a rather haphazard approach. It might sound romantic but a young, somewhat unworldly, man such as yourself, and I mean no offence, could fall victim to any number of crooks and flim-flam men. I know one or two businesspeople in the States. I will put you in touch. I make no promises, but they can at least give you some support while you seek employment.'

Joseph almost jumped out of his seat. 'You'd do that?'

'Let's resolve this case, then we can talk further. Promise you won't throw caution to the wind. I've always found it important to plan. With a plan there's still no guarantee of success but the outcome, should things go wrong, is often less disastrous.' He raised his hands to settle the excited Joseph. 'Let's return to the situation at hand. Did you hear or see anything at the time of the murder?'

'I was outside stretching my legs.'

'What time was this?'

'It must have been some time after four-thirty. I circled the house; I wanted to stay close in case we were called. I remember, on one occasion, hearing voices as I passed the ballroom, but when I looked in through a window, I could see very little happening. It was clear that rehearsals hadn't resumed.'

'Did you hear what was being said?'

'It wasn't loud enough for me to catch the words, but I feel certain it was an argument.'

'What makes you say that?'

'From the tone, it was apparent one of the people was angry.'

'Do you know who the voices belonged to?'

'One of the voices must have been Charles's – I could make out the back of his head. The other person...? I've no idea.'

'Did you notice anyone else as you passed around the house? You must have been able to see into many of the rooms. The library, sewing room, drawing room for example, all have windows to the outside.'

He thought for a moment. 'I remember seeing Bea Arling in the sewing room. Gino in the library and then sometime later in the sewing room with Bea.' He scratched his head. 'I think I saw everyone while I was on my walk. Shall I make a list for you? I can give it to you later, when I've had time to think about it.'

'Thank you, Joseph, a list would be extremely helpful.'

Joseph smiled with satisfaction. 'I'll hand it to you as soon as I can. I saw Bea in the garden at one point.

She wore her long blue coat. She looked worried; pacing around.'

'She was alone?'

'Yes.'

'You've been most helpful. That's all for now.' Fleming made his notes while the young man left the room.

'That was a very generous offer you made to Joseph,' said Nelson. 'A helping hand while in America is something he should be eternally grateful for.'

'I have seen too many lambs eaten by wolves not to offer help. I can see he would at some time try his luck and I would rather he didn't get eaten alive.'

'You assume he's innocent of this crime?' Nelson said with curiosity.

Fleming fixed Nelson with a steely gaze. 'I assume nothing. My offer, and this case, are entirely separate from one another. At this moment, young Joseph Timms is as likely of guilt as any other here. I will discover the truth, and perhaps prove his innocence, but until that point, he remains a suspect.'

Fleming got to his feet and stretched his legs and back.

'Who would you like next, Mr Fleming?'

'I will speak to Miss Bea Arling. Thank you, Nelson.'

CHAPTER FIVE

BEA ARLING

Bea Arling dabbed her nose with an embroidered handkerchief. Her white, smooth complexion reminded Nelson of a china doll. He felt her gloved hand trembling as he helped her to her seat.

'Thank you, Nelson. Goodness me, I wasn't sure my legs would hold out. I've been feeling quite faint,' she said.

'You're welcome, Miss Arling.'

Fleming poured a glass of water and passed it to her. 'I will be as brief as I can, Bea. It's been a long and trying day for us all.'

She nodded and sipped the water. 'Do you have any idea who's done this terrible thing?'

'I'm working on it. I assure you I'll find whoever did this and they'll be brought to justice.' He put aside his pen and paper, leaned back in his chair and folded his arms. 'I've wondered whether you have some insight into what has occurred here today.'

She shook her head. 'I have no idea.'

'It might be true that you know more than you realise.'

'I didn't see who did it, if that's what you mean.'

'It's important we look at the bigger picture. It's possible this was no spontaneous act. It could have been planned.'

'Planned?'

'You and I spoke before the murder, and you shared with me that you wished to end your relationship with Charles.'

Nelson sat a little straighter in the darkened corner of the room, his interest suddenly piqued by the conversation. He toyed with his empty pipe and tuned in.

'I did end it.' She choked back her upset. 'But it would seem he couldn't wait to move on... with Audrey.'

'You're referring to when you saw her leave his room?'

'Correct.' Bea stared at the embroidery on her handkerchief.

'Did you confront Charles about this?'

She shook her head.

'What about Audrey? Did you speak to her?'

Again, she shook her head. 'They certainly spent considerable time whispering together. I even saw him take her hand on one occasion. It would appear they were close.'

'We don't know for certain the nature of their relationship.'

'It's obvious. Charles was a monstrous womaniser. I see that now and feel embarrassed by my behaviour. I shared my heart with him and fell for his nonsense. He told me on many occasions he loved me and would leave Eileen so we could be together.' She shook the memory away and raised her head defiantly. 'That's behind me and now Charles is gone from all our lives.'

Fleming gave Bea a moment to compose herself. 'I had the impression at the time of our conversation there was more behind your reason to end things with Charles than you first confessed. Did I perhaps misread your feelings?'

Her eyes brimmed with tears. 'When I first had suspicions that he was carrying-on with Audrey behind my back, I discovered a letter from her to him in his jacket pocket. In it she asked to meet with him privately. It was after this that I saw only too clearly the way he looked at her, the way he spoke to her. I also discovered from Norman that he'd insisted she come to the island. When I confronted Charles about it, he brushed it off. He said he didn't owe me an explanation. It was quickly apparent to me then that he'd led me on with his flattery and lies, that I was just another notch on his bedpost. Like his wife, I too was betrayed.'

'Where were you when Charles died?'

'I was alone in the sewing room. I needed quiet between rehearsals. I read my lines and considered my future and the choices I'd made that had led me to where I am now.'

'What did you conclude?'

'That I must do better.'

'You knew Charles as well as anyone here.'

'I've realised I didn't know him at all. He was a cad and a liar.'

'But you knew of his mood of late? How did he seem?'

She sighed. 'He'd been very attentive; made me feel I was special. However, looking back, I can see that he'd become distracted. Discontent might be a good way of putting it. I pitied myself for a while. But I'm free of him now and should have walked away sooner. It's his wife who should really be pitied, not me. She's endured his ways for many years. I'm only sad I contributed to her pain and sorrow.'

'At the time of the murder, you were in the sewing room. Did you leave at any point or see anyone?'

'I don't think so. I wanted to be alone.'

'What about Gino?'

She hesitated. 'Yes. That's right. Gino was in the sewing room as well. I'm sorry, my mind's in disarray.'

'Of course,' said Fleming. 'Before this play, had you worked with any of the other actors?'

She shook her head. 'No. Not that I can recall.'

'Did you at any point leave the sewing room and go into the garden?'

'No.'

'Are you certain?'

'Quite certain.' She put her head in her hands. 'I'm finding it hard to think clearly at the moment. I need a break.'

Fleming and Nelson swapped glances.

Fleming rose from his seat. 'I think that will be all for now. You've been most helpful.'

When she'd left the room, Fleming sighed without realising he had done so.

'Something troubling you, Mr Fleming?' asked Nelson. 'I can tell you're fond of the girl.'

'I wonder if she's lying to me. She wasn't in the sewing room the whole time. I know this because Joseph and Gino told us as much. They both saw her enter the gardens.'

'From what I heard, neither of them sounded particularly certain.'

'Possibly you're right. Joseph mentioned her long

blue coat, but coats are much alike, especially in the fading light with a storm approaching.'

It was Nelson's turn to look puzzled. 'I've never understood why a woman would be attracted to a bounder like Charles Lockwood. From what I've heard today, he was a most unprincipled character with a reputation that preceded him. How does such a man impress a clearly intelligent and, if I might say, attractive young woman such as Bea Arling?'

'It's a complex matter of psychology. One that could well have a bearing on what's occurred here today.' Fleming tapped the table. 'We must continue our work. We'll speak to Norman Pottersmith next. Let's see whether he can shine a light on exactly how unpopular Mr Lockwood was and how many here today might wish him harm.'

CHAPTER SIX

NORMAN POTTERSMITH

Fleming waited. Nelson had made them both hot tea, which Fleming sipped as he studied the man in front of him.

Norman Pottersmith rolled up his shirt sleeves, then smoothed his horseshoe of greying hair. His bald head shone in the firelight. He seemed to be having trouble settling his six-foot-four frame. He leaned forward in his seat with his elbows on his knees. Deciding that was uncomfortable, he sat up and crossed his legs, then uncrossed them. Stood for a moment before sitting back down, then twisted to his right and stretched out his long legs in front of him. Finally, he was comfortable.

Fleming put his cup back on the saucer. 'Mr Pottersmith, Norman, I was curious about your relationship with—'

'With Charles? That's simple. I'm a talent agent. He's on my books. Has been for a couple of years. When nobody would hire him, he came to me. I found him work. I was helping to rebuild his reputation, and his career. It's what I'm good at.'

'How is it that you do that... rebuild a reputation?'

'That's the challenge and there are lots of elements to it. Don't think for one moment there's one quick fix. Charles Lockwood spent years trashing his reputation and that can't be rectified in one fell swoop.'

'Humour me. There must be some small clue you can give. I don't plan on becoming an agent myself. I'm quite fulfilled as a private detective.' He gave an encouraging smile.

'I'll share a little with you. I see no harm, I suppose. I'll do so in layman's terms so as not to confound you. If we take someone like Charles – a truly talented individual, at one time the darling of theatre goers and critics alike. The problem is that attention and adoration can become intoxicating. It turns to a belief that one is almost god-like, invincible if you will, that you can get away with anything. That, in turn, leads to poor decisions, less focus on craft. This arrogance leads to temptation, distractions, and stupidity. It's a recipe for disaster and I told him as much. My job is to remove the superfluous, refocus my client on what's important, and put him or her on the right path again.

Help them make better and smarter choices. Restore their confidence and reintroduce them to those who can put their career back on track.'

'Someone influential, like Randall Dobson?'

'Exactly like Randall.' He smiled from ear to ear. 'Randall did Charles, and me, a huge favour by taking a chance on him, but he also knows that if the gamble pays off, then he has a big name headlining his show. It worked well for all involved.'

'All except Gino Sadler.'

'That's unfortunate. Gino's a young man. He'll get other opportunities. I had to make a tough decision. Gino understands this. I'll make it up to him.'

'I assume that won't now be necessary. I imagine Gino will return to the lead role now Charles is dead.'

'That's being determined.'

'Of course.'

'I'm aware your business ran into difficulties some time back.' Fleming knew exactly when, but consulted his notes all the same. 'I fear you've not been so lucky in business over the years. Two years ago, you were in court for rent arrears on an office you occupied.'

'How do you know that? It hardly made the newspapers.' Then, rolling his eyes: 'Ah, of course. Lady Mabel Garfield most likely gossiped.'

'It was not Lady Mabel.' With a finger, Fleming softly tapped the side of his head. 'I make it my business to know and remember such things. I receive and study newspapers from around the world. I'm a detective not just of our United Kingdom, and I use little tricks of the mind to retain a considerable amount of information. I regularly receive a copy of the *Evening Standard*, amongst other papers, and a small notice was in a late edition. Names and faces are important. As well as their business dealings. I admit that fortunately I've also been gifted with an exceptional recall.'

Pottersmith sniffed. 'I've had my ups and downs over the years. My father taught me that if you get knocked down, you pick yourself up and keep moving forward. It's not a failure to make mistakes or have unexpected setbacks. It's the education of life. It's only a failure if you don't learn from it.'

'The education of life?' repeated Fleming.

'That's how I see it.'

'What of those affected by your failures? How would they see, for example, not receiving payment for rent on an office? They surely have their own bills to pay and family to feed?'

He sighed. 'I didn't come here to be lectured by you, Mr Fleming. I've been before the judge and those days are long behind me. And, if I may ask, what in Hades does any of this have to do with Charles's death?' He got to his feet and made to leave.

'Remain seated, please. I was merely trying to ascertain your current financial situation. It would seem you haven't always been a talent agent but have worn several business hats. A jack of many trades, perhaps?'

'Yes, I've had a few enterprises over the years. What of it? As for my financial status, that's none of your business.'

'You borrow money and are slow to repay your debts,' Fleming insisted. 'Owing or being owed money can be motivation for murder. How much did you owe Charles Lockwood?'

'Not much.'

'Did he offer to clear your debt with him if you rebuilt his career?'

'No.'

'Did he blackmail you?'

'No.'

'You offered to help him out of the kindness of your heart? Come on, Mr Pottersmith. How much did you owe him?' repeated Fleming.

'He offered to pay off a couple of my other debts in exchange for helping him.'

'Did he threaten you?'

Despite his eyes saying otherwise, Pottersmith said, 'No.'

'I think you owed him money, and he wanted his

debt repaid in full. You were in over your head, weren't you?'

Norman looked stunned. His eyes nervously darted between Fleming and Nelson. 'I see what you're doing here, but you're not going to pin his murder on me.'

'I'm not *pinning* murder on anyone. I'm merely in search of the truth.'

Norman jumped to his feet. 'I don't believe you. I have a criminal record, so it must have been me that did it. Is that right?'

'Please sit down and answer the question.'

Instead of sitting, Norman ran to the door and, without looking back, fled into the stormy night.

Nelson and Fleming stared at each other in disbelief.

'Well, blow me down! Does that mean he did it?' asked Nelson.

Fleming shook his head. 'It might suggest that he owed Charles money. It doesn't mean he murdered him. Though this foolish act does invite suspicion.'

Randall Dobson came to the drawing-room door. 'What on earth's going on? Norman'll catch his death of cold out there. He doesn't have an overcoat or even a hat with him. Should we go after him?'

'It would be both futile and dangerous,' insisted Fleming.

'What are we to do?'

'I suspect we'll find him sheltering in Nelson's boathouse come morning,' said Fleming confidently.

Nelson nodded. 'The boathouse is unlocked, and the stove's lit. He'll be fine.'

Fleming gestured towards the seat. 'Why don't you make yourself comfortable, Mr Dobson? I have a few questions for you.'

CHAPTER SEVEN

RANDALL DOBSON

The end of the slim panatela glowed red, like the heart of a volcano. Randall Dobson rolled it delicately between his finely-shaped fingers. 'A fine cigar is a work of art. This was rolled by hand the way a quality product of this nature should be. It's hard to believe one of these can now be made by a machine. Knocked out in its thousands every hour like a cheap cigarette. How does that advance humankind? It doesn't. It's another nail in the coffin of artistry. Much as cinema is to my industry. Theatre is like a fine cigar while cinema the cheap cigarette.' He pursed his lips and stared at Fleming. 'I didn't kill Charles. Mind you, there have been many times when I'd gladly have throttled him. I mean that in the figurative sense, of course.' His body shook as he chuckled.

'I understand you and he had quite a falling-out

many years ago,' said Fleming. 'That you swore never to work with him again.'

'I changed my mind.'

'What made you do that? What specifically? I know this is an important production. Why risk it with a man you despise in the lead role?'

Randall said nothing, simply puffed on his cigar.

Fleming could see this line of questioning would get him nowhere. Randall was an educated, powerful man who would say only what suited him. 'You've collaborated many times with Leonard Birch. I can see you two are very close. Do you consider yourself friends?'

'I love the man. I would do almost anything for him. His incredible talent as a playwright has brought us both success. I wouldn't be where I am today without him.'

'I'm sure he would say the same about you.'

'I'd hope so.'

Fleming saw the faintest of smiles. 'How did you meet?'

'I was a struggling actor, and he was just starting out. He couldn't get his play put on anywhere and so I suggested he write something for me. A one man show. He laughed and said I was mad. He must have thought about it some more though because, a few weeks later, he presented me with a genius of a script. A monologue called *The King's Last Breath*. It recounted the reminiscences of a dying king. All he had hoped for, all he'd achieved, the love of his queen, those he trusted, those who'd betrayed him, lands conquered, battles won and lost, his life's learning, mistakes, regrets. It was beautiful and poignant. The icing on the cake being that it was popular with audiences. He and I never looked back after that. We've worked together ever since.'

'What about Leonard's relationship with Eileen Lockwood?'

'What about it? It's none of my business what Leonard does in his private life.'

'Did it have any bearing on Charles getting the role?'

'None whatsoever.'

'Where are the flintlock pistols used in the play?'

'They're back in London. We didn't require them for the rehearsals. He wasn't shot with one of those. They're replicas. The bang of the pistol during the performance is done offstage. The pistol doesn't fire.'

'I wondered whether you keep any weapons in the house?'

'Absolutely not. The weapon used did not come from me, my property, or the theatre. Whoever it belongs to brought it with them, I can assure you of that.'

'Thank you. Where were you during the rehearsal break when the murder occurred?'

'I was with Lady Mabel in the kitchen and then we went into the garden to get some fresh air. She and I talked for some considerable time. She's a very interesting woman with many tales to tell.'

Fleming made notes. 'You were with her the whole time?'

'I think so. Yes. Until she went back to the house. I followed her shortly after.' Randall pointedly looked at the time on his Cartier Santos watch. 'I've nothing to gain from Charles's death, in fact his demise leaves me with a real headache. This sets me back weeks, you realise that, don't you? And once the newspapers get hold of the story, it's going to be on everyone's lips. I've invested a considerable amount of my own money into getting this production off the ground. I should never have listened to Pottersmith.'

'What do you mean by that?'

Randall frowned. It appeared he'd perhaps said more than he'd intended. 'He was very persuasive; keen that Charles have the role. I couldn't tell you why. I've since wondered whether Charles had something on him. I'm not suggesting Pottersmith is capable of murder, of course. I do know, however, that he's someone I don't enjoy doing business with. He always has an angle of some kind. I deal with him because I have to. Not because I want to.'

'He has something on you?'

Without his having to say so, Fleming could see he did.

'If I were a gambling man, I'd say Charles's death will somehow lead directly back to his association with Norman Pottersmith.' He leaned forward in his seat. 'There's something else.'

'Yes?'

'I know for a fact that Pottersmith owns a small pistol.'

'You've seen such a weapon?'

'Not here on the island. He showed it to me during a meeting one time. He laughed about needing it for protection. He was worried his unsavoury past would catch up with him one day and he wanted to be prepared.'

'He carried it for protection?'

Randall nodded. 'That's what he implied. I don't want to point the finger but, if I were you, I'd search his room. I think you'll find what you're looking for there.'

'You should have told me this immediately.'

Randall looked confused. 'It only just came to mind. I remembered it during the course of our conversation. It's no great mystery. I have a lot to contend with just now.'

'You have so much on your mind that you neglect to inform me that Pottersmith carries a weapon?' Fleming lightly thumped the table in frustration. 'You've withheld vital information!'

He shrugged. 'I withheld nothing. I remembered only at this precise moment.'

'You might have put other lives in danger.'

'Oh, I'm *so* sorry. Of course, I should have solved the case for you. It would have saved us all a lot of time and we could have forgone this...' Randall nonchalantly waved his cigar, '... this little charade.'

'You've disappointed me, Mr Dobson. I'd hoped you were a better man than this. I'm not sure what kind of game you think you're playing, but I take the crime of murder seriously. We have a killer amongst us and you've seen fit to act in your own self-interest. I find that unforgivable.'

'Charles Lockwood is no great loss to the world. In fact, when we discover who killed him, I might even shake that person's hand. If it's transparency you want, then I'm glad he's dead. With one or two exceptions, perhaps, I think it's safe to say most of us here tolerated him. We were forced to.'

Without another word, Randall Dobson got to his feet and flounced out, slamming the door behind him.

Nelson and Fleming looked at one another.

'An emotional bunch, these actors,' said Nelson.

'I must agree,' sighed Fleming.

'However, that was enlightening, to say the least.'

'Indeed it was. I wanted him to believe I was angry. Our suspects must not be allowed to think this investigation is akin to a walk in the park, and they can simply be vague with their answers or withhold information. He'll return to the others and no doubt mutter words of discontent.'

'My, but you're a canny one,' said Nelson admiringly.

'Perhaps.'

'Should we search Pottersmith's room?'

'Though a search of his room would be prudent, there's no rush. If indeed he's our killer, then he's unlikely to have left the house, leaving the weapon behind. I'm certain the culprit discarded the pistol. My instinct tells me that is what our mystery person whom we met outside in the rain was doing. Whoever it was panicked. They were not expecting to have company in the garden.'

CHAPTER EIGHT

LADY MABEL GARFIELD

'I cannot tell you how sorry I am to have brought you into this most undesirable situation,' said Lady Mabel Garfield. 'I feel quite embarrassed.' A lock of grey hair had broken free from the bun piled atop her head and it hung, unnoticed, behind her ear. Her soft, thin, finely aged face looked tired.

'There's no need,' said Fleming. 'It could be argued that I'm the right man, in the right place, at the right time. Who else among us could investigate such a crime?'

'I suppose you're correct. However, promise me as a friend, if I ever again ask you to join me on a remote island in the middle of a storm, you'll decline!'

Fleming chuckled. 'Where's the adventure in that?'

Lady Mabel pulled her fur tippet closer around her

neck. Seeing she looked cold, Nelson threw another log on the fire.

'I know you have questions to ask, Henry, and of course I'll cooperate in any way I can. Treat me as you would any other suspect. I won't take offence. I understand that you have a job to do, and I insist you do it without the hindrance our friendship might be.'

'That's most understanding, Mabel. In that case, I'll jump right in. We've known each other a long time and I'm aware you own a pocket pistol. A weapon you picked up in New York while working there several years ago. Where is this weapon now?'

Lady Mabel lifted her beaded purse from her lap by its delicate gold chain, turned the filigree clasp and presented the weapon.

Nelson raised his eyebrows.

Fleming took the pistol from her and examined it.

'Has this weapon been out of your sight since you arrived on the island?'

'It's been in my purse the whole time I've been here. I've had no reason to take it out.'

'Has the purse been out of your sight?'

'I've put it down several times. It's been in my room while I perform. I keep it in a bedside drawer when I sleep.'

Fleming put the pistol to his nose and smelled it. His eyes narrowed. The small weapon sat in his open palm, its silver-plated barrel gleamed, and the mother of pearl grip felt cool and smooth.

'What is it?' asked Lady Mabel.

'Mabel, this weapon has been recently fired. It has a very distinct smell.'

'But that's impossible.'

'It's far from impossible. You yourself have told me that the purse in which you carry this pistol has been out of your sight on more than one occasion. I think it's fair to say we have our murder weapon.'

'But you must understand that I didn't do it,' insisted Lady Mabel.

'If you wish to clear your name, you must continue to answer my questions as honestly and precisely as possible.'

Lady Mabel's voice trembled. 'Of course. I'll be truthful.'

'Would you consider yourself friends with Charles Lockwood?'

She hesitated. 'No. Not really. He was a difficult man. Not somebody I would ordinarily associate with except through my acting work.'

'Have you socialised with him?'

'Although I've known Charles for years, we haven't socialised all that much. I've chatted with him at a party recently. I once had dinner with him to discuss a play. It was purely business and, in the end, I declined the offer.'

'Yet you knew him well enough to insist Bea Arling stay away from him?'

'It wasn't my place to insist on anything. I did suggest she act wisely. He was a married man, known to behave caddishly. I was concerned for her reputation. I'm old fashioned that way.'

'Did you confront Charles about his relationship with Bea?'

'I took him to one side at the end of rehearsals one lunchtime. I asked him to leave her alone.'

'How did he respond?'

'I could smell alcohol on his breath, and his tone was entirely dismissive and mocking. He told me to keep my nose out. He reminded me that Bea was a grown woman, and said he was fond of her.'

'How did you respond to that?'

'I reminded him that he was married. That Eileen was a lovely woman and that his behaviour was outrageous. He as much as laughed in my face.'

'How did that make you feel?'

'Angry. Upset. Worried for Bea.'

'Why did you take such an interest in Bea's welfare?'

'She was staying with me. As you know, Henry, I never had children of my own and I felt protective of her. Motherly, I suppose you might say. Though she acted to the contrary, she wasn't very worldly, and somewhat naïve. Maybe I was being an interfering old lady, but I couldn't help myself.'

Fleming nodded thoughtfully. 'I understand. With age comes knowledge and experience. It's sometimes hard not to want to impart that hard won wisdom. Even when it's not necessarily wanted.'

He paused before continuing.

'Did you see anyone near or close to your purse? Or your room? Has the pistol been in your purse the whole time?'

'I don't recall seeing anyone. And, as I've already said, I only ever keep the pistol in my purse. Never anywhere else.'

'Besides me, does anyone know about the pistol?'

'I don't publicise it but at the same time it's not a secret. It's a deterrent. I think it's better that people know I can defend myself should the need arise. The streets of London can be unforgiving. Especially for a woman.'

'Where were you at the time of the murder?'

'After the rehearsal ended, I took a little walk. I had some soup. I read for a while. I haven't been sleeping well lately, so I took a nap. It was all quite uneventful.'

'Did you speak to anyone?'

'Yes, I did. I talked to Randall for a while. I met him in the kitchen and then we went into the garden.'

'Can you remember what you talked about?'

'Not really. He was very distracted. Worried about the future of the play. He's invested his own money in it.'

Fleming referred to his notes and his interviews with Randall and Pottersmith. 'Did he talk about anyone else?'

She shook her head. 'No. He seemed worried and extremely concerned about being ready for opening night.'

'He wasn't angry or frustrated?'

'Not at all. Quite normal, in fact. We parted after our chat, and he seemed happier. He said I'd put his mind at ease. I went back into the house.'

'What about Randall?'

'I'm not sure. Though I believe shortly after I headed towards the house, he followed.'

'In which direction did he head?'

'He'd mentioned he needed to get things ready in the ballroom for the next rehearsal. I assumed that's where he was going.'

'Where did you go after your walk?'

'I wanted to go back to my room. I passed Leonard and Eileen talking in the hallway. They fell silent as I passed.'

'Did you catch any of the conversation?'

'Nothing. They simply looked at me and smiled. I went to my room and closed the door.'

'I see.' Fleming pinched the bridge of his nose. 'Finally, I wondered how well you know Audrey Warren?'

'I've chatted to the girl, but I couldn't say I've got to know her. I'm aware she works for Charles as she told me she'd been doing some secretarial work for him. I'm not quite sure what that entailed, but she's a pleasant and polite young lady.'

'Secretarial work? Is that what she told you?'

'Definitely. She told me she was newly qualified and was sent to Charles via an agency.'

'Thank you. I think that will be all for now. If I have further questions, I'll come and find you.'

Lady Mabel looked hesitant. 'Did I do all right, Henry?'

'I learned a lot. You did very well.'

'My pistol. Will you be keeping that?'

'It will be evidence that I'll pass along to the police in due course.'

'I see.' Worry crept into her eyes.

'Don't fear. I'll do my best to have this case resolved before the police arrive. The pieces of the puzzle are already beginning to reveal a picture of this crime.'

There was relief in her voice. 'It's a blessing you're here. I feel my life is in the safest of hands.'

'Don't mention what we discussed in this interview, nor the weapon. Especially the weapon.'

The latch clicked as the door closed behind Lady Mabel.

Nelson stared out of the window. The storm had quietened and, for the time being, it seemed the thunder and lightning had moved out to sea. The rain had settled into a steady, hypnotic pitter-patter. 'I know she's your friend, but it's quite damning the murder weapon was in her possession. If you were the police, I feel certain she'd have been arrested.'

'Then it's fortunate I'm not the police. As a private detective, I'm able to expand my mind to other possibilities. Ask questions and consider scenarios beyond the scope of most detectives. A police officer is trained to follow a routine course of action. This stifles thought and imagination, both of which are essential to a successful outcome. How else can we consider all the avenues that might lead to a crime such as this? As distasteful as it might be, one must occasionally use devious means.'

Nelson shuddered.

CHAPTER NINE

AUDREY WARREN

I t was a good ten minutes before Audrey Warren stopped crying. Fleming waited patiently. When she wiped her eyes for the final time with her handkerchief, he passed her a glass of water.

She took a sip and placed the glass on the table in front of her. 'I'm not sure I can be of any help. Each time I think I have my emotions under control, I recall what happened and the tears come flooding back.' Her nose and cheeks were pink, her wide blue eyes bloodshot, her wild blonde curls held back from her face with a jewelled headband.

'I quite understand. It must be such a shock.'

'I'd only just met him. We were getting to know each other. Until recently, he'd been nothing more than a picture in my mind.'

'You were hired as his personal assistant?' asked Fleming. 'For secretarial duties?'

She gave a curious smile. 'That's the official role I was given to stop tongues wagging, but I was rather more than that.'

'I see,' said Fleming. 'Where did you meet Charles?'

'My first contact with him was by letter. I wasn't sure how he'd react to my getting in touch with him, so I wrote a brief note to introduce myself and things blossomed from there. When the time was right, we decided it would be easiest if we met at the train station. We lived some distance apart and so it was decided I'd catch a train to London. He kindly paid my fare on each occasion. He said it was the least he could do.'

'Did you go somewhere from there?'

'Sometimes we had tea and cake in the station café, or we would walk and talk then have a drink and dinner at a nearby hotel. The time seemed to fly past. We had so much to say to each other. I thought our conversations might be awkward, but it was just the opposite. I'd talk for ages, and he'd listen. Then he'd do the same. It was a dream come true. When he and I were together, I was filled with a joy I'd never experienced before.'

Nelson snorted with derision, then cleared his throat when Fleming shot him a disapproving look.

'Did he talk about his wife, Eileen?'

'Oh, yes. We talked a lot about her. He explained that though married, they led quite separate lives. They'd had many ups and downs over the years, but she was his one constant and best friend. He relied on her completely and couldn't imagine his life without her. I thought that was incredibly sweet. I told him about my mother. How she'd loved me and how my childhood had been happy and comfortable. I told him lots about her and, of course, he was very interested.'

This time Nelson couldn't hide his incredulity. He and Fleming looked at one another with disbelief in their eyes. 'If you don't mind my saying,' said Fleming carefully. 'You speak as though your relationship with Charles is perfectly normal. Though it's not my place to judge, he's considerably older than you. You write to him. You arrange to meet him. You talk with him for hours on end. You dine with him at hotels. He's a married man. Did you think at any point that your relationship with him was wrong? That an unattached young man of your own age might be more appropriate?'

It was Audrey's turn to look bewildered, her blue eyes narrowing. 'I'm sorry? I don't understand. What do you mean?'

Fleming said flatly, 'Let me be clear. Charles Lock-wood was old enough to be your father.'

Audrey chuckled softly. 'But Charles Lockwood *is* my father!'

'I beg your pardon?'

'Charles is my father,' she repeated firmly. 'I found letters when my mother passed away. She and my grandparents brought me up on their farm. I sought him out after her death because I wanted to know him.'

'Charles is your father?' Fleming seemed quite mystified.

'Now, just like my mother, he's gone, too.' She nodded and wiped her nose with her handkerchief. 'I assumed you knew. I'm the last person you're speaking to, so I imagined someone would already have informed you.'

Nelson, still utterly bemused, removed a hip flask from his back pocket and took a long restorative swig.

Fleming slumped back in his seat, his mind whirring at this new revelation. He shook his head. 'It appears either Charles told nobody or, as is more likely, if he did, they kept it from me. I assume the role of personal assistant was simply a guise to enable you to stay close to him without arousing suspicion.'

She nodded proudly. 'It was my idea. I wanted to spend more time with him and when I heard he was coming to the island, I asked if I might accompany him.'

'That's ingenious of you.'

'You thought we were... having a relationship?' She wrinkled her nose.

'I'm sorry,' said Fleming. It was apparent Audrey was oblivious to Charles's unsavoury reputation. 'I should have realised. I'm angry with myself for not seeing this sooner.' He got to his feet and began pacing back and forth.

'Are you all right?'

'This takes my thinking in a whole new direction. I must go over it all again. Piece by piece.' He turned to Audrey. 'When did you first contact Charles, your father?'

'Only three weeks ago. I sent a letter and it took him a week to reply. He said he'd needed a few days to consider what to do for the best. He said he quickly realised he had to meet me; I'm his only child.'

'There are two questions I must examine. Did anyone discover your relationship but choose not to reveal it? And does it have any relevance at all to his death?'

Audrey gasped, horrified. 'You think I might have inadvertently caused his death?'

Fleming took her hand. 'To want to know your father when you discovered this secret is perfectly natural. Whatever we find, you must never blame your-self. I want you to promise me.'

She nodded. 'However tragically brief our time together, it has helped me understand who I am.'

'I'm only sorry you didn't have more time with him. You have my word. I will uncover the truth and reveal to you the reason for his death.

'Your embroidered handkerchief?' Fleming gestured towards the handkerchief in Audrey's hand. 'I noticed the initials are not your own. EH. It's a small detail, but details matter.'

Audrey scrunched the handkerchief in her hand before slipping it into her sleeve. 'Eileen gave it to me. I've been very upset these last few days. I wasn't as prepared with such items as handkerchiefs as I should have been. She was the first person Charles told and she's found the fact of my existence hard to bear. She and I have talked, and I hope we'll be friends, but the news has been difficult for her.'

Fleming assisted Audrey as she left the room. He closed the door behind her and turned to see Nelson placing another log on the fire. He moved the embers with a fire iron.

'I can't see how you'll make sense of this,' said Nelson. 'All we've learned is that Charles was disliked by pretty much everyone. Possibly even his own wife. On top of that, we find Audrey's Charles's daughter. A revelation his wife chose to keep secret. Any one of these guests could be lying.' He turned and looked at Fleming thoughtfully. 'Yet, if I was a betting man, I'd say it was Norman Pottersmith. Let's face it, only the guilty have reason to run.' He scratched his head. 'But then again, your good friend Lady Mabel was carrying the murder weapon.' He took another sip from his hip flask. 'Mind you, seems to me his wife has more reason than anyone to kill the swine.' He slumped down in a chair. 'It's a mess. My mind goes round and round in circles.'

'I'll sleep on the matter,' said Fleming. 'Quite often a good night's sleep reveals answers to many of the more difficult questions.'

Nelson frowned. 'How can you sleep at a time like this?'

Fleming took out his pocket watch. It was after midnight. 'I must. The mind needs its rest. It's a muscle and if it's not rested, it cannot work at peak performance. Thank you for your assistance today. It was greatly appreciated. I will ensure a room is available to you tonight.' Fleming collected his notes and, after a word with Randall about accommodation for Nelson, he bid them all goodnight and vanished upstairs to his room.

As was his habit, he locked his door.

ACT THREE

THE CURTAIN OF TRUTH DRAWN BACK

CHAPTER ONE

A NEW DAWN

Fleming had risen at daybreak. With the rain ceasing for a while, he'd left Damson House and now stood watching the boathouse. The small stone building was a few metres away from the shore, at the top of steps carved into the rock and part-way up the cliff between the beach and Damson House.

A faint spiral of smoke rose from the chimney. Fleming suspected Norman Pottersmith was holed up inside.

In his hand, Fleming held a heavy walking stick. He'd brought it with him for protection. It had been the mention of Pottersmith owning a pistol that had spooked him and caused him to bolt. If he chose to use the pistol, rather than talk, then the walking stick would offer scant protection.

Fleming took a deep breath and walked up to the front door.

He knocked twice.

'It's open,' yelled a voice. It was barely audible over the sound of the crashing waves below.

Fleming pushed open the door.

Inside, Pottersmith stood beside a stove. He held a pan of boiling water. 'I was making tea. Want one?'

'That would be nice,' said Fleming, relieved.

'There's no milk.'

'Black tea is fine.'

Fleming watched as Pottersmith stirred the cast iron tea pot and placed a lid on top.

'My natural instinct of wanting to run got the better of me yesterday. I presume you've searched my room.'

'I didn't find your pistol.'

'I tossed it over the cliff. As soon as you mentioned he was shot using a weapon similar to my own, I knew I had to dispose of it. With my history, I'd surely be the prime suspect. Now there's no evidence against me.' He added sugar and passed Fleming a cup of tea. 'No proof we even had this conversation.'

Knowing Pottersmith wasn't about to brandish a weapon, Fleming relaxed a little. 'I need you to come back to the house. It's important this investigation is brought to a close.'

'I'm comfortable here.'

'That might be so, but Nelson will be travelling to the mainland this afternoon. Tomorrow he'll return with a police detective. It's important we're all together when he arrives. Otherwise, you look more guilty.'

Pottersmith was silent while he thought about it. 'I'll return on one condition.'

Fleming's eyes narrowed. 'Tell me.'

'Promise me that if anything happens to me, you'll make sure Audrey's looked after.'

'You knew she was his daughter?'

'Charles confided in me. He was immensely proud of her, said she was the most beautiful thing he'd ever seen. He thought she'd make him a better, more responsible man.' He chuckled. 'I told him I doubted that, but would hope for the best. I really think he was making an effort. He was even trying to make things right with Eileen.'

'He and Eileen were working things out?'

'It was early days. He wasn't sure she'd forgive him quickly, but he planned to do what it took. It was important to him that Audrey saw him as a person she could respect.'

'I can understand that.'

'Will you look out for her?'

'I'll do my best. You have my word.'

After finishing their tea, they shut up the boathouse and returned to Damson House.

Slumped in an armchair, Gino drank down a glass of whisky and immediately poured another. He wedged the bottle beside him and, glass in hand, he pointed an unsteady finger at Joseph Timms. 'I'm glad he's dead. Pottersmith did us all a service. Let's face it, the world's a better place without him.' He put two fingers together like the barrel of a gun. '*Bang!*' he said.

'For heaven's sake, keep your voice down. You don't mean that, and it's far too early in the day to be drinking.' He eased the bottle away from Gino and put it back in the drinks cabinet.

Gino grabbed Joseph and pulled him to him. 'I've been watching you. You're up to something.'

'Don't be absurd. You're drunk!'

'I'm not drunk enough.' His dark eyes narrowed. 'I see the way you look at Audrey. You like her. Don't you?'

'She's a friend.'

'What about Bea – you like her, too?'

Joseph finally wrestled the glass out of his hand and escaped his grasp. 'I'm going to make you a coffee. No more drinking.' He held up the key to the drinks cabinet and showed Gino, before slipping it into his pocket. 'I'm taking the key with me!' He left the drawing room and bumped into Fleming, who was on his way to the kitchen.

'I suppose you heard all that?' said Joseph.

'I think the whole house heard it.'

'He's maudlin and trying to drown his sorrows. I'm not sure what's got into him. I've never seen him like this before.'

'We're all a little on edge. It would seem our fears manifest themselves in different ways.'

Joseph nodded. 'I'm not sure drinking would help me feel better.'

Fleming smiled at the young man. 'You deal with the pressures of life in a different way, I think. You're a person who likes to busy himself in good times and bad. You're keen to be helpful, which is why you now look after Gino. You look after Audrey and Bea, too. You have a protective nature.'

'I suppose so. I can't bear to see people in distress. I'll always do what I can to prevent that.' He blushed. 'I'd better go to the kitchen. I need to make coffee and get Gino sobered up before he says or does something he'll regret.'

'I was going that way. I'll come with you.'

The kitchen door was slightly ajar. Inside, Fleming and Joseph heard voices. Joseph was about to push open the door when Fleming placed a restraining hand on his arm.

'Once we get off this island, why don't you come and stay with me?' said Leonard. 'We've talked about it many times. I hate to think of you alone at a time like this. I'd make sure you were looked after.'

'Stop! Just stop.' Eileen pushed away his hand. 'I don't want you mollycoddling me every two minutes of the day. I need space. I know you mean well, but I can't breathe with you constantly pressuring me. I'll give you an answer. My answer's no. I don't want to live with you. In fact, I never wanted to leave Charles. It was you who wanted that. I know he was a swine. I know he was unfaithful. He gambled and drank and treated me like dirt, but deep down we loved each other. He was special. A free spirit, and he was mine. When I was in his arms, there was nowhere else in the world I'd rather be. Nobody else ever came close to making me feel that way. I repeat. My answer is no. I will not betray what I had with Charles. Not now. Not ever. I would rather be alone than dilute my memory of him.'

Leonard's mouth dropped open. He paled and blinked in disbelief. 'What about everything I've done for you? The plans we made?'

'You made plans for us. I listened. I never agreed to

anything. Everything you've done was in your own self-interest.'

'You made me believe we had a future.'

'No, Leonard, I never made any promises. Whatever you think we had is over.'

'I know you don't mean that.'

Eileen got to her feet. She placed her hands on the table and leaned towards him, scowling. 'When I leave this island, I never want to see you again. There, is that plain enough for you?'

Leonard jumped up, the wooden chair scraping on the tiled floor. It crashed loudly to the ground. He snatched her wrist and twisted it.

'You're hurting me!' Eileen cried.

Fleming threw open the door. He and Joseph stared at Leonard in disbelief.

'What's happening here?' barked Fleming.

Leonard released Eileen and stormed from the room.

Eileen rubbed her wrist. 'It's nothing.'

'On the contrary. It would seem Leonard has quite a temper after all,' said Fleming.

'I provoked him.'

'That's no excuse,' said Joseph. He ran a tea towel under a cold tap and passed it to Eileen. 'For your wrist,' he said.

'Thank you, sweetheart.' She suddenly burst into tears.

Joseph helped her to a seat.

When she had regained her composure, Fleming asked, 'What did Leonard mean when he said "What about everything I've done for you? The plans we made?"'

She shook her head. 'There was a time when I wanted to leave Charles. Leonard offered to help me start over. Since then, I've been clear that I loved Charles and would never leave him. Very recently, Charles and I had talked of the future together.'

'How did you feel about Audrey?' asked Fleming.

Joseph looked confused.

Eileen took a long, deep breath. 'She's Charles's daughter,' she explained.

Joseph was completely shocked, his mind quickly piecing together all the moments he'd seen Audrey and Charles together. He staggered to his feet. 'Please excuse me.' He rushed from the room.

Eileen placed the cold, wet tea towel on the table and turned to Fleming. 'Audrey told you?'

'Yes.'

'I was pleased for Charles. For us. He changed once he'd met her. He wanted us to be a family. As soon as he learned of Audrey's existence, he shared the news with me. I was upset and angry at first. Who wouldn't be? Then I softened. I soon realised she was the chance he and I needed. The glue that might finally keep his feet on the ground. He was going to move back to our house in the country when we returned to the mainland. He asked if I minded Audrey joining us for a while. I told him I'd think about it.'

'Why don't you talk to Audrey? I'm sure it would do the two of you good.'

She sighed wistfully. 'I've been meaning to. It's what Charles would have wanted.'

CHAPTER TWO

GRACE AND FAVOUR

On the cliff top, a small group had watched Nelson's boat head out to sea. He carried with him a letter from Fleming which he was to hand to the local police station on the mainland informing them of the situation on Damson Island and requesting the immediate assistance of a senior police detective.

The group had then gathered at a table on the terrace outside. Bea Arling led the barrage of questions being asked of Randall Dobson.

'I don't have all the answers,' said Randall eventually. 'I'm hoping the play will continue with Gino taking over Charles's role as lead.'

Gino tried not to smile but was finding it difficult. He winced, closed his eyes, and pinched the bridge of his nose as the alcohol began slowly and painfully to leave his system.

'We'll then need to figure out a few other things, but I see no reason why, with a lot of hard work, we still can't open on time.'

'I don't want any more lines than I already have,' said Joseph. 'I can't think straight as it is. I'm not sleeping properly.'

'It feels wrong. As though the play has been cursed,' said Bea.

'Stop that sort of childish nonsense at once!' demanded Lady Mabel.

'I simply don't think I can continue,' said Joseph. 'The reality is that it won't just be Charles we're missing. Someone among us killed him and the police will discover who that is. Then we'll be yet another person short. Who'll want to see a play where cast members have either been murdered or imprisoned?'

'You'd be surprised,' said Pottersmith. 'The publicity certainly won't do any harm. It could help ticket sales no end.'

Lady Mabel shook her head disapprovingly. 'I'd rather you didn't repeat what you just said in front of me again. A man has lost his life. It's improper to suggest the play will profit from that fact.'

'As usual, I'm only saying what the rest of you are thinking,' said Pottersmith.

There were side glances and mutters.

'I still don't understand why Fleming was so

convinced Nelson had nothing to do with the murder. He was the only stranger among us. He barely ever said a word to anyone. He was hardly the friendliest person I ever met.'

'I thought he seemed polite,' said Joseph.

'You give everyone the benefit of the doubt,' said Gino. 'Not everyone is what they seem.'

'You're quite right,' said Fleming. All heads turned his way as he joined the small group.

'Did you find what you were looking for?' asked Randall. 'I saw you down on the beach. You appeared to be searching for something.'

Fleming could feel Pottersmith's eyes on him. Fearful he would mention the pistol he'd tossed over the cliff.

'My search was, for the most part, fruitless. As I had suspected it would be,' said Fleming. 'No matter. The answer to Charles's murder doesn't rely on physical evidence alone.'

'You sound as though you know who murdered him,' said Lady Mabel.

Fleming had a twinkle in his eye. 'Almost,' he said. He put out an arm and Lady Mabel joined him for a walk through the garden. When they were a good distance away from the group, he turned to her. 'Tomorrow I will present my findings.'

'So you do know who murdered Charles?' She looked concerned.

Fleming's face was full of sadness. 'I do. It gives me no joy to finally understand what's happened and why.'

'You must do what you have to.' She turned to him, her eyes full of sorrow. 'She would be proud of you. Of what you've become.'

Fleming took out his pocket watch and opened the case. Inside was the likeness he always carried with him. He showed it to Lady Mabel.

'She was beautiful. She loved you so very much.'

'Not a day goes by when I don't wonder what could have been. My life would be very different had her life not been cut so short.'

'It was a tragedy, but Grace's death was no mystery, Henry.'

Fleming said nothing. He didn't have to. His eyes revealed what he really believed. He slipped the pocket watch back into his waistcoat, then reached into his jacket and took out his precious ornate tin.

'You still carry it with you?'

'It was her last gift to me. She'd filled it with sugared almonds. Sweet treats to help me think. I take my mind off the problem and often the solution appears. Now, Mrs Clayton fills it for me.' He opened the tin and offered the candied peel inside to Lady Mabel, then took some himself. 'These little rituals keep her alive for me. I carry her memory wherever I go.'

'If it's what you need, then there's no harm. Letting go of the past isn't always the answer. I hear people say we should learn to move on, but I don't necessarily agree. There's comfort in what we know and remembering the people we've loved. The very act of remembrance can bring sadness, of course, but also immense joy. They may have gone from our day-to-day lives, but while they're in our hearts, they're always with us. They've shaped our past and they'll shape our future.' She paused. 'Never letting go will make it difficult for you ever to find love.'

'I'm not sure I could ever love like that again.'

Lady Mabel looked sad at this declaration. 'At least give it some thought. Grace wouldn't have wanted you to be alone forever.'

They walked in silence for a while. Now the storm had passed, they enjoyed the warmth of the sun on their backs.

CHAPTER THREE

TIME TO FACE FACTS

Henry Fleming had forgone breakfast, opting instead for a pot of tea in his room, which he'd poured, but not touched. It was now lukewarm. He sipped it, grimaced, then drank down the remainder in one go.

He put on his jacket and straightened his tie. He checked the time on his pocket watch. Ten-twelve a.m. It was time. From the dresser, he scooped up the ornate case filled with candied peel and slipped it into his jacket pocket. He patted it twice. Taking a deep breath, he went downstairs to where the guests had been instructed to assemble at precisely ten a.m. Having assumed there would be stragglers, he'd arrive late. There was usually at least one who'd want to make a point and be deliberately tardy. He felt sure if it was anyone, it would be Gino Sadler. He wasn't wrong. He met Gino on the stairs. He was rubbing his head and carrying a large cup of black coffee. They walked into the ballroom together. It had been the scene of the crime and now it would be the place where he revealed the killer. It seemed fitting somehow. He waited for Gino to take a seat beside Bea. Looking around the room, he noted all were present.

Interestingly, Leonard and Eileen sat apart, neither looking at the other. Joseph sat with Audrey. Gino and Bea were together with Lady Mabel. Norman and Randall sat close, but not too close. The conversation lulled. Eyes turned to Fleming without his needing to say a word.

'I've gathered everyone here this morning for the very solemn task of discovering who murdered Charles Lockwood. Husband to Eileen. Renowned stage actor. A man who, some might say, was difficult to get along with and, I think it's fair to say, had many vices. What is clear is that at least one person among us found themselves motivated enough to kill him. A pocket pistol was placed at the back of his head and the trigger pulled.'

Audrey sobbed loudly.

A sigh and a stifled yawn from Gino Sadler. He sipped his strong black coffee.

Fleming immediately turned his attention to Joseph Timms. 'Your positive attitude, protective nature, and willingness to ensure others are happy hasn't gone unnoticed,' began Fleming. 'It's apparent you enjoy making sure those you're fond of are treated well. You give of your time, and your empathy knows no bounds.'

He smiled cautiously. 'I do what I can. It's in my nature and it's not something I can resist.'

'It would appear you have a bright future ahead of you. Whatever path you decide to take.'

'I hope so.'

'I learned from Leonard that you've written several plays. Some of which have promise. Leonard suggested you have quite a gift.'

Joseph looked in Leonard's direction.

'It's true. With some guidance, I feel sure you could do well,' said Leonard.

'This made me wonder why you were so keen to travel to America. It's clear you have talent both on and off the stage.'

'I simply feel there are greater opportunities across the pond.'

'It would be a great loss,' added Leonard. 'Although I can see how the lights of Broadway might be a great draw for a young man such as yourself.'

'Thank you, Leonard,' said Joseph. He held Audrey's hand. The young pair comforted each other.

'I understand from our conversation that your

plan is to finish the play, then catch the first boat you can?'

'I must honour my commitment to Randall. He's put faith in me. I can't leave the production now. It would be wrong of me.'

Gino Sadler laughed and tutted. 'No offence, but it's not like you'd be missed, Joey boy. I mean, you're not exactly a linchpin in this show, are you?'

'What a horrible thing to say,' said Lady Mabel.

'It's the truth.'

'He's right,' said Joseph. 'It's a small part. Hardly memorable. But it's *my* small part, and it's important to the play.'

'You're right,' said Randall. 'We're grateful for your commitment and enthusiasm.'

'Suddenly, I'm the bad guy for speaking the truth? When is everyone going to stop pussyfooting around? Am I the only one here willing to say out loud anything that resembles how we're all feeling? Can't anyone else feel the weight lifted with Charles gone? He was mean. To everyone. He cared for nobody except himself. Eileen, you of all people should know that.'

Fleming stepped in before Eileen answered. He feared what she might say and cause the situation to escalate further. 'Gino, you've made your feelings clear. You were no fan of Charles, and he was no fan of yours. I understand that your words are built on a foundation of mutual dislike. It's also clear you have a motive for wanting him dead.'

'Nonsense.'

'You're an ambitious and proud man. It must have been crushing to have had the lead role snatched from you. To be replaced by someone you despised and who routinely belittled you. Called you out on every little mistake. Scoffed at your abilities.'

'It never bothered me.'

'For an actor, you're an unconvincing liar.'

'Everyone here accepts I was treated badly. Not only by Charles, but by Randall and Pottersmith. The lead role was mine. It's what I was promised. I'll admit I felt angry. Who wouldn't? I certainly wouldn't kill because of it, though.'

'What if we were to add the fact that he then took away your chance with Bea? It's true that you have feelings for her? I imagine you felt outraged. You knew his track record. You must have wondered if he took her just because he could and because it was clear how much it would hurt your pride.'

Gino looked at Bea, his face flushing. 'I'm not going to lie. I'm fond of Bea. He was not only toying with her, but with me, too. It made me despise him even more. However, I repeat, it wasn't enough to make me kill him. I might rant and rave, but when it comes down to it, I couldn't have harmed him.'

'A man who went behind Charles's back to Randall and Pottersmith to complain about him so publicly would be a fool to then kill him. I also have a witness who saw you in the sewing room with Bea Arling at the time of the murder.'

'Exactly,' said Gino. 'I might flap my mouth too loudly and too often, but I'm not a killer.'

'On this point, I will agree. Your arrogance does you no favours.'

Gino was sweating profusely. 'I can accept that. I can work on my attitude.'

Fleming turned next to Bea Arling. 'Even though you were unaware of it at the time, your relationship with Charles caused some considerable upset for those who cared for you, and eventually yourself.'

'I never meant for any of it to happen. I've said repeatedly how ridiculous I feel to have been swept along by the romance of it all.'

'Romance?! You foolish hussy!' blasted Eileen. 'You'll understand the pain you caused if you're ever a married woman. You mark my words, every time your husband's head is turned, it'll feel like a knife in the heart. I only hope for your sake that he never strays. And don't tell me you're sorry because those are hollow words and far, far too late. They mean nothing to me.'

Fleming waited for Eileen to finish, then returned his attention to Bea who, unable to look Eileen in the eye, was looking down at the floor. 'I know from speaking to you that even though you knew it was wrong, you cared for Charles. He led you to believe his marriage was effectively over and promised you a life with him.'

'I'm now aware he said the same thing to many women.'

'You were even more hurt when you assumed he'd ended his relationship with you and started one with Audrey.'

'What was I supposed to think? I saw her leaving his room.'

'You were angry.'

'I was deeply hurt.'

'I wondered if you were upset enough to murder him?'

'No. And even if you think I was capable of it, I had no pistol with which to do it.'

'Yet, you knew where one could be found.'

Bea glanced at Lady Mabel.

Fleming held Lady Mabel's pocket pistol over his head for all to see.

There were several gasps.

He slipped the pistol back into his jacket pocket.

'You were a woman scorned, Bea. You knew where to find Lady Mabel's pistol. The only question that remains is whether you had the opportunity. You claimed to have been in the sewing room at the time the murder took place. Joseph Timms saw you there with Gino through the window. He, and Gino, claim also to have seen you in the garden.'

Joseph looked at her out of the corner of his eye. 'I did see you, Bea. I'm sure of it. I saw you both in the sewing room and then you were alone in the garden.'

She shook her head. 'I don't remember.'

'Two witnesses saw you at the time of the murder,' said Fleming. 'Unless they're both lying, which seems unlikely.'

Fleming turned next to Lady Mabel Garfield. 'Before the murder took place, you claimed to be in the garden.'

'That's correct.'

'I have a list from Joseph, and he claims to have seen you. He does not mention that you were talking to Randall Dobson.'

Lady Mabel looked concerned. 'He's mistaken.'

CHAPTER FOUR

MIMI WILDER

'Joseph must have forgotten quite what he saw,' said Lady Mabel. 'It must be an oversight on his part.'

'I wasn't expecting it to be necessary to remember all the details. I did my best,' explained Joseph.

'Lady Mabel and I talked for some considerable time in the garden,' said Randall Dobson.

'We met in the kitchen. Randall made us tea. We then went outside to continue our conversation.'

Fleming went back to his notes from the interviews. 'You claim Randall was anxious about the play?'

'Correct,' said Lady Mabel.

'I would agree,' said Randall. 'I had my concerns before Charles's death. As you might well imagine, I'm even more worried now.'

'With the controversy surrounding Charles in the lead role, it's not too much of a stretch for me to assume, Lady Mabel, that you were questioning Randall's decision? You knew how unreliable Charles could be.'

'Everyone questioned the decision,' said Lady Mabel. 'At my time of life, I hope to be around people whose company I enjoy. When Charles joined us, the whole dynamic changed. I explained to Randall how the general atmosphere had been upset and wondered if that was perhaps why he wasn't getting the best from his cast. Hardly anyone was enjoying the experience.'

'I assume this fell on deaf ears?'

'That was my feeling after our conversation,' said Lady Mabel. 'I wasn't necessarily expecting change. I simply wanted to explain how I felt.'

Fleming paused and waited for Randall to respond.

'It's complicated. I know my decision was unpopular,' said Randall.

'Then why do it? Surely everyone here would like an explanation.'

'I don't need to explain myself. It's my production. I have the final say.' He tried to avoid looking at Norman Pottersmith but couldn't.

'The decision wasn't yours though, was it?' said Fleming. 'It was down to Mr Pottersmith. In fact, he's the one who insisted Charles was hired. You had no choice but to go along with it. It's possible that after you agreed, you regretted the decision and decided the only choice you had was to remove Charles from the play. Permanently. You can either tell us what Pottersmith has on you that forced you to hire Charles, or you can wait and I'll learn the truth once we return to the mainland. For your sake, it would be better if this was dealt with here and now.'

Pottersmith shook his head. 'Don't do it!'

Randall looked resigned, pinched the bridge of his nose and sighed loudly. 'It was many years ago. A young actress fell from the stage and died as a result. She and another actor got into an argument, there was some pushing and shoving and she fell, hit her head on the edge of the stage. I lied to the police, told them she'd caused problems in the past and was a known troublemaker. The other cast member backed me up; between us we painted a very grim picture of her. I've never forgiven myself.

'Charles was there; he must have told Pottersmith.'

'Charles helped cover it up?' asked Fleming.

'Yes, he did.'

'It was *you* who convinced Charles to keep his mouth shut,' said Pottersmith. 'You couldn't jeopardise your *precious* play, could you?'

Randall jabbed a finger at Pottersmith. 'You're a liar and a parasite! Look where we've ended up and all thanks to you!'

'Stop your pathetic whining. Unlike you milksop, I have a spine. You fanny about while I make the decisions you can't stomach.'

'I don't need you, Pottersmith. You've caused me nothing but distress.'

Fleming paced the room, listening to the bickering and accusations, watching and learning. Looking for further proof, if any were needed, that he wasn't mistaken in his conclusions. His thumb stroked the pocket watch he could feel in his waistcoat. This case was different than usual – he was having to feel his way, and he didn't like it. Trapped on the island, he was unable to look into the suspects' background and probe the way he normally did. He also had little time. Once the police arrived, it was out of his hands. On the wall of the ballroom was a huge clock. Judging by the tide this morning, he thought maybe he had another hour before Nelson and the police arrived. Probably less.

Fleming silenced the two men and stared at Pottersmith. 'It says here on my paper from Joseph that you were seen in the drawing room at the time of the murder.'

'What does he know?' Pottersmith snorted dismissively.

'Joseph was walking around the house at the time of the murder. By looking through windows and doors, he was best placed to locate everyone.'

Joseph nodded. 'I did see everyone. I know where everyone was.'

'Well, who's a clever boy?!'

'Yes, I was in the drawing room. I opened a bottle of something and had a drink.'

'You went to a lot of effort to get Charles into the play. You'd already secured Gino as the lead and the only reason you'd change that is if you had no choice. This could mean that Charles had something on you and was pressuring you to get him on board. Something from your past perhaps, a crime of some sort, but I don't think Charles was in any position to be threatening you, was he?'

'No, he wasn't.'

'In which case, it's money. You owed Charles money and he wanted it back.'

Pottersmith looked sheepish for the first time. 'With interest,' he said. 'I borrowed from him when a low-life from my past threatened to break my legs if I didn't pay. In exchange, Charles wanted his money and his career back within a year. At the time, I had little choice, but I hadn't realised the extent of the Charles Lockwood problem. I'd vastly underestimated how difficult it would be to get him cast in roles. It was as if he'd dedicated years to rubbing up the wrong way anyone with influence within the theatre. The man was a walking disaster. I had my work cut out, but I had an advantage over most agents – I lacked scruples.' He chuckled. 'We made quite the double-act.'

'It was during this double-act you discovered Randall Dobson's secret.'

'Exactly so.' Pottersmith smiled gleefully. 'To help Charles, I needed to know everything about his past. After a few drinks, he had no problem spilling his guts. He was desperate to act again, even more desperate to be liked. It was like a drug to him; he craved the spotlight. It was during one of these drunken conversations that I learned about the actress who fell from the stage, and Randall's involvement in covering it up. Her name was Mimi Wilder. After a late-night show, when the theatre was all but empty, she'd arrived on stage looking for Charles. He told me she was throwing all kinds of wild accusations at him – admittedly most of which were probably true. He tried to walk away, to laugh it off, and that's when she went crazy, slapping him and kicking out. He raised an arm to defend himself and, somehow, she tripped and fell off the stage. The poor girl died in his arms. Charles panicked. He knew how it looked. Randall didn't want a scandal in one of his theatres, so he and Charles covered up the truth. After that, Randall vowed never to work with Charles again. He wouldn't have done either, if I hadn't persuaded him otherwise. In order to get Charles back on the stage in a meaningful way, I suggested I'd release the story of the young woman's death to the press. I know several journalists who'd eat up this kind of stuff.'

'I don't understand. Surely that would have damaged Charles's career, as well as Randall's?' said Lady Mabel.

'Charles's career was already dead in the water. He had nothing to lose,' said Fleming. 'It was unlikely there would have been any criminal charges because it was an accident, but it was scandalous, nonetheless.'

'You're correct,' said Pottersmith.

'I, on the other hand, had everything to lose,' explained Randall. 'I not only finance and direct shows, but I've also invested in the buildings themselves in central London. If a show of mine gets shut down, or there's a downturn in takings, I lose out massively.'

Fleming addressed the group. 'Mimi Wilder certainly deserved better from Charles, Randall and Pottersmith. Despite how I feel about their actions, it's apparent they wouldn't benefit from Charles's death. On the contrary, they were invested in seeing him succeed. Lady Mabel has an alibi because she was with Randall at the time. We shall move on.'

All eyes now turned to Eileen Lockwood and Leonard Birch. Many in the room knew of their friendship and had wondered how deep it went. Had they plotted his death?

CHAPTER FIVE

POTENTIAL WITNESSES

F leming keenly observed everyone in the room.

Eileen Lockwood didn't physically need to get up and move away from Leonard Birch; the tension between them was palpable. Her body language said it all; she wanted nothing to do with him. She glanced towards Audrey.

Fleming had noticed that, out of the corner of her eye, Audrey had been watching Eileen with a curious look on her face. Was she in need of Eileen's reassurance? He wondered if they had spoken since Charles's death.

Fleming turned to Leonard. 'Like everybody else here today, Joseph Timms kindly provided me with your whereabouts shortly before the murder. He noted Eileen was in her room upstairs and that he saw you, Leonard, knocking on her door.'

'That's right,' said Joseph. 'I'd popped upstairs to my room at the end of the hall. That's when I saw Leonard talking to Eileen through the door.'

'I didn't see you,' said Leonard.

'You were busy. Eileen didn't want to talk to you.'

Fleming continued. 'Then Lady Mabel saw you both conversing in the hallway when she returned to her room shortly before the murder was discovered. This corroborates both your stories. I'm also aware that Eileen was planning to make a fresh start with Charles. Something which I'm now convinced she genuinely considered possible.'

'That seems inconceivable to me,' said Leonard. 'You can have no real idea what she's had to put up with over the years. His drinking, gambling, mood swings, womanising, general need for attention every minute of the day and night.' He shook his head with disapproval.

'For God's sake, stop! I've had enough,' Eileen snapped forcefully. 'You tell me you know what I need, but you *don't*. I know you care, but you don't understand the whole story.'

Leonard hung his head. 'I'm sorry. Why don't you tell us why you'd want to give him another chance to make it work? I'm sure we'd love to hear it, when we all knew you'd be better off without him.'

Eileen looked at Audrey and then pointed at Fleming. 'He knows,' said Eileen. 'So does Audrey.' She got up and sat beside her, reached out and took her hand. Both women smiled at each other, eyes brimming with tears. She whispered to Audrey, 'Tell them, sweetheart.'

In Audrey's hand, Fleming noticed the same handkerchief embroidered with the initials EH she'd had before. She'd told him Eileen had given it to her. It was an easy step to assume that Eileen's maiden name began with H, hence EH. Perhaps it had sentimental value which was why she still had it after so many years of marriage. Audrey looked around at everyone. After a deep breath, she said, 'Charles was my father. He and my mother were in love but not married. She discovered she was pregnant and her parents, my grandparents, sent her away to have me in secret. After Mother recently passed away, I discovered the truth in letters she'd written to Charles but never sent. I found Charles and wrote to him. To my astonishment, he wanted to meet me. I finally knew my father, and was no longer alone.' She dabbed at a tear. 'No sooner did I find him than he was taken from me.'

'Hang on. I don't understand?' said Gino. 'You're his daughter? Charles was your father?'

'Yes, he was,' said Eileen. 'He and I discussed it at length and decided we wanted to be a part of Audrey's life. We were never blessed with children of our own. Audrey changed both our lives.'

'Why did you not tell me this?' demanded Leonard.

'Charles wanted it kept between us until we were ready. He and I felt we needed to get to know Audrey, and she to know us, before it became public.' She squeezed Audrey's hand. 'I want you to know that you're not alone. Though Charles has gone, if you want me, I'm here for you. My feelings haven't changed. It's what Charles would have wanted, and it's what I want, too.'

Audrey was lost for words. She mouthed a thank you.

'How lovely!' said Lady Mabel, dabbing at her eyes.

'You're his daughter?' repeated Joseph weakly. 'His daughter!' He hung his head, and clenched his fists.

Fleming watched Joseph closely. He had a fair idea what was going through his head. He walked over to the young man. 'There's a reason you know where everybody was at the time of the murder. You needed to know you'd be alone with Charles for the split second you needed. You saw Leonard outside Eileen's room because you went to Lady Mabel's room while she was outside talking to Randall. Bea had told you of the pistol Lady Mabel carried in her purse and you took your chance. Having found it, you went directly to find Charles. He was alone, here in the rehearsal hall. You walked up behind him and pulled the trigger.

You then returned the pistol to Lady Mabel's purse, only just managing to do so before she arrived back at her room. You then resumed walking around the house until Charles's body was discovered by Randall.'

There was shocked silence, in which one could have heard a pin drop.

Joseph stared at Fleming, the realisation dawning in his eyes that he had no place to hide.

Audrey looked at Joseph in disbelief. 'Is this true?'

Joseph's mouth opened and closed. 'I made a mistake,' he said. 'I thought you and he...'

'He killed Charles out of a misguided need to protect you. He's fond of you and wanted to save you from Charles. He, like others here, thought Charles had broken off his relationship with Bea to pursue you.'

'I'm sorry,' muttered Joseph. 'I really thought he was going to break your heart the way he had Bea and Eileen's. I couldn't stand by and let him do that. I don't know what got into me. I'm not a violent person. It was a moment of madness. If I'd known the truth, I would never have done it. Why on earth didn't you tell me, Audrey? If only you had told me.'

He broke down, no longer able to speak. His body trembled, and he appeared to visibly shrink into himself in front of everyone's eyes.

'Eileen Lockwood said something very interesting

to me,' said Fleming. '"... no rational person would wait to be surrounded by so many potential witnesses to commit a murder." The interesting thing about that statement is that Joseph attempted to do just that. He used the fact that he knew the whereabouts of every single guest as his own alibi. Unfortunately, he inadvertently drew my attention to himself. By making sure nobody else was near Charles at the time of the murder, he exposed his own wrongdoing. He knew precisely where each of you were and picked his moment.'

'I'd hoped there would be enough confusion that I could get away with it,' admitted Joseph quietly. 'I'd planned to return to the mainland and immediately catch a boat to America. I wanted to get as far away from all this as possible.' He sank his head into his hands. 'What have I done?'

'It's a real-life Greek tragedy,' said Lady Mabel. 'So much heartbreak and sorrow.'

CHAPTER SIX

MRS CLAYTON'S FINE BAKING

Fleming was slowly pacing outside Damson House, mulling over the case, when he heard a voice behind him.

'Well, when they said "private detective", I wondered if I'd find you here on Damson Island, Fleming, but dismissed it as highly unlikely!'

Fleming turned and saw the familiar figure of Inspector Carp. 'Inspector Carp, we meet again.'

'Indeed we do,' agreed Carp, shaking Fleming's hand. 'From what I understand, you have things wrapped up pretty watertight. You'd better bring me up to speed.'

'This has been a sorry business, Inspector. Perhaps, in the privacy of the drawing room, I can take you step by step through proceedings as they unfolded.'

When Fleming had finished explaining, the two men emerged from the house, an exhausted looking Carp scratching his head. 'One thing I was wondering, Fleming, if you don't mind my asking? What are you doing here, hob-nobbing with all these arty-farty theatrical types?'

Fleming frowned. 'I was invited by Lady Mabel Garfield. She's an old friend of mine.'

Carp smoothed his moustache and raised an eyebrow. 'Lady Mabel, eh? I'm a great fan. I don't suppose you could introduce me?'

Fleming and Inspector Carp were joined by Nelson. 'We'll soon need to weigh anchor before the tide turns, Mr Fleming,' said Nelson.

'Ah, well,' said Carp, disappointed. 'Another time perhaps?'

'I will leave the formalities of this case in your capable hands, Inspector. You know where to find me should you have any questions.'

'Right you are,' said Carp. He straightened his shoulders and headed back inside.

Fleming was about to turn and leave when he noticed a young constable escorting a hand-cuffed Joseph past the front of the house. Head down and shoulders sagging, Joseph raised sorrowful eyes towards Fleming.

Fleming stopped the constable and spoke softly. 'I shall speak on your behalf in court, Joseph. I'm not sure how much good it will do, but I feel I must explain to the judge and jurors a little of what has occurred here and of your character. Though you acted with the best of intentions, you made a fatal error of judgment and there is no doubt it will cost you dearly.'

Joseph was unable to speak. He gave the faintest of nods before being moved on.

'You're feeling sorry for the lad,' said Nelson.

'Sorry's not the right word, but I certainly feel something for his plight. He acted on impulse, out of a mistaken need to protect Audrey. His actions were ill-conceived, and he will pay heavily. Possibly at the end of a rope.'

'What will you do now?'

'Yes, what do you have planned now, Henry?' asked Lady Mabel, who had joined the two men.

'I'll return to Avonbrook Cottage. Walk my dog. Assess the needs of my garden. Try not to overindulge in Mrs Clayton's fine baking. Read my books and newspapers and await my next investigation.'

'What about yourself, Mabel?' asked Fleming.

'I'm staying on for a few more days. Randall has asked if I can help him salvage the play. He somehow thinks my experience and clear head can be of some use. I quite like the thought of being useful, so I agreed.'

'As promised, Mrs Clayton and I will attend the opening night,' said Fleming.

'I look forward to seeing you then.'

They said their farewells and went their separate ways.

Nelson helped Fleming aboard.

Audrey, wrapped warmly in a fur coat, stood on the clifftop holding Eileen's hand. The two women, brought close in grief, leaned on each other for support.

Fleming raised an arm in solemn farewell. There was little comfort he could offer, but his fervent hope was that they would be able to forge a future together.

Mrs Clayton handed Fleming a slice of carrot cake. As usual, it was enormous and three times what he required.

'You've lost weight,' she commented. 'I'm surprised you could think, let alone solve a case, while not eating. I worry about you when you're away and you don't do much to allay my fears. Were there no meals on this island? No cook? Any staff at all?'

'I was only gone a matter of days.' He patted his stomach. 'I can assure you I'm in no danger of fading away.'

'If you're going to be like that, you won't be wanting that cake of yours. I'm sure Skip would enjoy it.'

Skip's ears pricked up, tail wagging at the mention of his name.

Mrs Clayton playfully tried to take away the plate of cake.

Fleming moved it out of her reach. 'I've truly missed your wonderful baking and delicious cooked meals.'

Somewhat mollified, she turned towards the kitchen, only to return a few moments later with a tray of tea. 'Once you've settled in, Lewis would like to speak to you about the allotment. Rabbits have decimated the late lettuce, and he wants to discuss the next quarter. I've put a pile of letters in your bureau drawer. I need to go into town this Saturday to buy a new outfit. I can't attend the theatre otherwise. I'll also need to book an appointment with Sheryl to get my hair done. She's a marvel, as you know. I'll ask her to visit. Who'll look after Skip while we're away?'

Fleming chuckled at this torrent of words. He patted Skip. 'I'd be delighted to take you into town in the Austin 7 and buy you a new outfit. Ask Sheryl as soon as you like. When I speak to Lewis about the garden, I'll see if he'd be kind enough to once again take care of Skip while we're in London.'

Mrs Clayton appeared satisfied. 'That's very generous of you.'

'I know you're attempting to take my mind off the Damson Island case. It caused me sleepless nights and in the end it was a painful discovery. I'll admit I was fond of Joseph.'

'I've gathered that,' said Mrs Clayton. Uncertain what to say or how to ease his sadness, she pointed to the cake. 'Eat up,' she instructed. 'I know you'll do your best for the young man when you speak on his behalf in court. You can do no more than that. You know as well as I do, you can't help everyone.'

'The law's the law, and he killed a man,' said Fleming as if to convince himself. 'Even if that man was a thoroughly despicable character, Joseph must be punished.'

'Quite so,' said Mrs Clayton. She poured tea into a fine china cup, added two sugars and placed it on the small table beside Fleming.

At Mrs Clayton's insistence, he forked another piece of cake into his mouth and savoured it. 'Delicious! Thank you, Mrs Clayton. This cake is exceptional.'

'Now finish that, then go and see Lewis about the gardens. The best thing you can do is busy yourself until your next case comes along. I've a feeling there's something quite challenging right around the corner, and you need to be ready for it.

Thank you for choosing this Henry Fleming mystery. I hope you enjoyed it and will return for A Deadly Venetian Affair.

Henry Fleming Investigates
Murder in Fulbridge Village
The Mystery of Watermead Manor
Death on Damson Island
A Deadly Venetian Affair

Short Story
The Theft of the Kingsley Ruby

Inspector James Hardy
Chilling British Crime Thrillers

Caution: This series contains occasional strong language, moderate violence, and mild sexual references.

Knife & Death

Angels

Hard Truth

Inferno

Killing Shadows

Don't Go Home

Inspector Hardy Box Set, Books 1-3

Inspector Hardy Box Set, Books 4-6

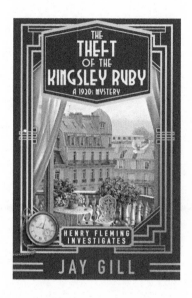

Never miss out, sign up to the newsletter mailing list on my website, and join me on Facebook, Instagram and more.

Jay Gill Newsletter
www.jaygill.net

Facebook Author Page
facebook.com/jaygillauthor

Instagram
instagram.com/jaygillauthor

Twitter
twitter.com/jaygillauthor

TikTok
tiktok.com/@jaygillauthor